A DRESS FOR CURVES

THE SCOTTISH BILLIONAIRES

M. S. PARKER

BELMONTE PUBLISHING, LLC

This book is a work of fiction. The names, characters, places and incidents are products of the writer's imagination or have been used fictitiously and are not to be construed as real. Any resemblance to persons, living or dead, actual events, locales or organizations is entirely coincidental.

Copyright © 2022 Belmonte Publishing LLC

Published by Belmonte Publishing LLC

THE SCOTTISH BILLIONAIRES READING ORDER

SEASON 1:

Alec & Lumen:
Prequel
1. Off Limits
2. Breaking Rules
3. Mending Fate

Eoin & Aline:
1. Strangers in Love
2. Dangers of Love

Brody & Freedom:
1. Single Malt
2. Perfect Blend

SEASON 2:

THE SCOTTISH BILLIONAIRES READING ORDER

Baylen & Harlee:
Business or Pleasure

Drake & Maggie:
At First Sight

Carson & Vix:
A Dress for Curves

Cireon & Christina:
Bad Press

ONE
CARSON

Most days, I loved living in New York City. The people. The energy. The diversity.

Today was not one of those days. The entire week had been hot and muggy, not unexpected for mid-August, but this morning had started with a brown-out, which meant there was a chance the electricity would go out.

At least I had a generator somewhere here in my studio should it be needed.

I went to the lounge in the back to retrieve a bottle of Shannon's whisky. Grabbing three glasses with the bottle, I carried them out to the studio, which took up most of the four-thousand square foot space. Baylen McFann and his girlfriend, Harlee Sumpter, sat on the modern black leather couch, waiting for me.

We had been discussing the upcoming launch of a new type of bra that Baylen and his ex-partner had designed. I had agreed to help with the launch in

America and the finishing touches on the designs. Though I didn't know him well, Baylen was a close friend of Alec, my eldest brother. Their friendship went back to their days at the University of Glasgow, and they, along with two other friends, had stayed in contact despite Alec living in Seattle, while the other three had stayed in Scotland.

I poured each of us two fingers of my other brother, Brody's best whisky. It was a little early in the day, but what the hell. We were celebrating.

"To take on the fashion world by storm," I said with a smile.

"Which is *not* something I ever thought I'd say." Harlee took a sip of her drink, and her smoky blue eyes widened. "Wow."

"Aye." Baylen chuckled. "The McCrae boys know their alcohol." He savored his mouthful, then added, "Brody outdid himself with this one."

"He's quite pleased with the batch himself," I said wryly. "Then again, he usually is."

Baylen laughed, his blue eyes sparkling. "I thought all you McCrae's had that attitude."

It was my turn to laugh. "You're right. We tend to be a self-confident lot."

My sister's face popped into my mind, and my good humor dissipated. I still blamed myself for not noticing Maggie's abusive bastard of an ex-boyfriend had torn her down the entire three years they'd been together. She'd finally gotten away from him this past spring and was only now finding her confidence again.

We could have lost Maggie forever if it hadn't been for Drake, her savior and fiancé.

"Did I say something wrong?" Baylen's concern pulled me out of my head.

I forced a smile to return. "Not at all."

"I heard you designed Bryne Dawkins's wedding dress," Harlee said before the moment of silence could get awkward.

"I did." I felt a burst of pride. "She and my youngest sister, London, worked together, and when Bryne's dress was destroyed, London recommended me."

"I remember the story and the pictures. It was gorgeous, especially considering how little time you had to work."

"Thank you."

"And, on behalf of non-model-sized people everywhere, thank *you* for designing beautiful clothes for all sizes and shapes." She tapped her glass against mine and took another drink. "All without using labels like 'plus-size' or 'husky.'"

I shrugged. "I've never much liked labels of any kind."

"Me either." Harlee grinned.

Considering she had dark blue streaks in her hair, multiple piercings, and at least two tattoos, I wasn't surprised. She certainly didn't strike me as someone who enjoyed being told what to do.

"I've been meaning to ask…." Baylen shifted the subject. "Do you do casting calls to find models? I would assume you can get the typical model through an agency, but what about other types?"

"I do sometimes have open casting calls," I said. "In fact, I've been searching for a while to find the last model I need for this season's designs, and you never know where you'll find the perfect model. Even on the street."

"Like you just see someone and ask them if they want to be a model?" Harlee asked. "How does that *not* sound like a line?"

I laughed. "Oh, I've had plenty of people who thought it was."

"I'd imagine those were some interesting conversations," Baylen said with a grin.

"You have no idea. I once asked a six-and-a-half-foot construction guy if he'd ever considered being a model."

Baylen's eyebrows shot up. "How did he respond?"

I had to laugh at the memory. "The guy said he might consider it, as long as he could keep his clothes on because even a man as pretty as me didn't do it for him."

Harlee squinted at me and shook her head. "Pretty? Really?"

"You don't think another man could find me pretty?" I arched my brow.

"Nope," she said. "Hot? Yes. But not pretty."

"You think he's hot?" Baylen scowled.

"C'mon," Harlee said, "look at him. If you were the slightest bit heteroflexible, you'd be all over that."

I almost choked on my whisky as Baylen laughed.

"I only have eyes for you, babe," he teased.

"Is that so?" She pulled him up against her.

The temperature in the room went up ten degrees as they stared into each other's eyes before the chime from a cell phone interrupted. Baylen dug into his pocket and pulled out his phone.

"Sorry." He glanced at the screen, then at Harlee. "If we want to get dinner before the show, we should probably get going." He turned to me. "Anything else we need to discuss?"

"I think we've covered everything for now," I said. "Whatever comes up, we can take care of it later. You two, enjoy your time in New York. Let me follow you out."

But before we reached the door, it flung open, the sunlight almost blinding us. All I could see was the silhouette of a woman standing in the doorway.

TWO

VIX

Soie et Velours was a cute and expensive boutique owned by Karen Devereaux, a woman in her mid-forties who had made her fortune by marrying and later divorcing a wealthy, older businessman. I've worked here with Susanna Ballance since I arrived in Manhattan two years ago. Not only did she help me get this job, but she also took me in as her roommate the very first day we met. She was a fantastic person.

"Where's the mannequin?" Susanna asked when I came out from the backroom empty-handed.

"It's not there," I said with a sigh. "I even checked the boxes with the holiday decorations."

"Fuck. Karen will be pissed if we don't get the display set up today."

"Any ideas?" I asked as I moved to the desk and straightened the items. "Because I can't think of anywhere else it might be."

The bell over the front door rang, and I took a few steps in that direction.

Wonderful.

Karen Devereaux had not only graced us with *her* presence, but she also brought her twenty-year-old daughter, Brietta. As frustrating as Karen was, Brietta was worse. I usually believed the best in people, but it was tough with the two of them. They constantly tested my patience.

"I hardly think my mother pays you to stand around," Brietta said, scowling. "Working off some of those extra calories you've been consuming wouldn't hurt."

As hard as it was, I ignored her.

"Where's my display?" Karen Devereaux asked, her eyes narrowing.

"We haven't found the mannequin," Susanna said. "We've searched everywhere."

"Obviously not," she snapped. "Because, if you had, you'd have found it." She dropped her purse and opened the back door. "If I come out again in a minute with the mannequin, you're both fired."

Susanna and I exchanged looks. Unless there were a secret room where the mannequin was hiding, Karen Devereaux wouldn't find it.

"Mom!" Brietta went after her mother, her voice an irritating whine. "We have to go!"

"Then come help me," Karen Devereaux snapped.

The look on Brietta's face said she didn't want to

do anything that could be construed as work, but she didn't dare disobey her mother.

Potential customers arrived, which gave Susanna and me something to do while waiting for the pair to return. A couple of minutes later, they came back without a mannequin. I suppressed a grin at the matching looks of annoyance on the women's faces.

"Brietta and I have an important social engagement to attend," Karen Devereaux announced. "And since I've now wasted all my time dealing with this," she waved her hand to include everything around her, "I won't be able to handle an urgent matter." She zeroed in on me. "So you're going to do it."

My eyebrows shot up. "I'm going to do what, ma'am?"

She retrieved a manila envelope from her bag and held it out to me. "Do not–under any circumstance–fold, crease, or wrinkle this."

I took the envelope carefully, still unsure what she wanted.

"Take it to Carson McCrae's design studio in Greenwich Village." She rattled off an address as she tucked her fancy handbag under her arm. "Make sure you give it to Carson McCrae and him alone. Not to an assistant or anyone else, understood?"

I nodded.

"I can't believe you're trusting *her* with this," Brietta said, her lips twisted into an unattractive scowl. "If you really believe in me and my career, we should go there ourselves."

Karen Devereaux gave her daughter a sharp look. "We don't want Carson thinking he's your only opportunity. Showing up in person makes you look desperate."

Karen Devereaux turned to me. "Why are you still here? Get over to Carson and don't return until he has that in hand." She pointed at Susanna. "And you. Find a new mannequin somewhere. Now."

Neither of us argued, and I gave Susanna a nod before heading out.

It was a warm day, but I walked rather than take a cab since the address was only about ten blocks away. I didn't mind the heat and wanted to stretch my legs. Besides, the sounds of the city still fascinated me.

When I finally arrived in front of Carson McCrae's Designs, I'd long regretted my decision to walk. The humidity had my sundress sticking to me, and I was eager to get inside.

I opened the heavy door, and as I stepped into a spacious, modern warehouse-style studio, I almost bumped into a trio of people. The woman was pretty, with the attitude I associated with native New Yorkers. The man at her side was handsome, with auburn hair, but the other man caught my attention.

He had burnished curls, wild in a way that made me wonder what it would be like to run my fingers through them. Then his baby blue eyes met my gaze, and I felt like all the air went out of the room.

"Can I help you?" he asked, giving me a charming smile.

"I'm looking for your boss." I smiled back at him.

"My boss?" he asked.

"Not to be rude," the other man said with an apologetic smile, "but Harlee and I need to get going."

"Of course," the man said. They shook hands, and he turned back to me. "Sorry about that, Miss...?"

"Teal," I said. "Vixen Teal."

I waited for the inevitable joke about my unusual name, but all he did was ask, "You want to speak to my boss?"

"Yes. *My* boss asked me to give this to Mr. McCrae." I held out the envelope. "And you can call me Vix, by the way."

"And your boss is?" He took the envelope, looking at both sides as if searching for a name.

"Karen Devereaux," I said and snatched back the envelope. "And she gave specific orders to give it to Mr. McCrae directly."

"Oh." His smile widened. "And you're her assistant?"

"No, I work at her store. She asked me to deliver this."

"Asked?" He raised an eyebrow. "I don't think Karen Devereaux has ever *asked* anything of anyone."

His accurate observation made me laugh. "She is my employer, so her telling me what to do is her prerogative."

"I doubt playing delivery girl is in your job description." Then he corrected himself. "Sorry. Delivery *woman*."

"It's all right," I assured him. "No offense taken."

"My sisters would disagree," he said with a self-deprecating grin.

"Do you have many of them?" I asked.

"Sisters?" He looked surprised at my question. "You really have no idea who I am, do you?"

"You're not Carson McCrae's assistant?"

A charming smile revealed his dimples as he gestured to the studio area. "Not exactly. I'm the designer behind all this."

"You're kidding. Carson McCrae doesn't make his own designs?" My curiosity got the better of me, and I took a few steps further inside.

He stopped me with a gentle touch on my arm. "I'm Carson McCrae. Nice to meet you, Ms. Teal."

The blood rushed to my face. "I'm so sorry, Mr. McCrae. I thought you were much—"

"Older?" He gave me a crooked smile that eased my anxiety. "I get that a lot." He pointed to a series of sketches sitting on easels. "So, do you like what you see?"

They were all incredible, but one, in particular, caught my eye. It was a stunning cocktail dress. "I like this. It's rare to see high-end designs for women who aren't stick figures."

"Everyone should have access to clothing that makes them feel good about themselves," Carson said, walking over to the sketch I was admiring. He looked at it and then back at me, a speculative look in his eyes.

"How comfortable are you wearing little clothing in front of people?"

"That's an odd question to ask a stranger," I said with a smile.

"I'm always looking for new models," he said. "Besides, we're not really strangers. I know where you work, and I know your employer. You know that I'm a legitimate designer and where I work."

I studied him for a moment, searching for any hint of impropriety, but found none. "What, exactly, are you asking me?"

"I'd like you to model for me." He gestured toward the sketch. "This dress, and maybe a new line of bras. What do you say?"

This was crazy. Was Carson McCrae hitting on me? I mean, it had to be a line that he was using. I'm certainly the furthest from a runway model with these hips. Logic told me to say no and walk away. But curiosity has always gotten the better of me, and I shouldn't let fear stop me. I never had before.

Logic be damned.

THREE
CARSON

Before the door closed behind Vix, I tossed the envelope into the trash. No way in hell was I ever working with Brietta Devereaux. By herself, she was bad enough, but when you hired Brietta to model, you got her mother too, and that was *way* too much drama for my taste.

As I walked back into the main part of my studio, I stared at the note with Vix's number on it. I didn't know what'd made me ask her. Sure, I thought she could be a good fit for what I needed, but hiring amateurs came with its own set of problems. Modeling was hard work, standing on your feet for hours without breaks. Typically, I'd ask potential models to come in for measurements and tests, like finding out if she could walk gracefully in high heels.

Why had I skipped my usual way of doing things? Maybe the conversation earlier with Baylen and Harlee about finding undiscovered talent from the street had been playing in the back of my mind? Or had it simply been because she was gorgeous, and I'd felt an instant attraction?

Hardly. The most beautiful people in the world constantly surrounded me in various states of undress, yet I couldn't deny there was something different about her. I'd felt it from the moment she'd walked into my studio.

That didn't mean she'd be a suitable model, though. Far from it.

I needed to use my head, not other parts of my anatomy.

No harm done. If Vix weren't a perfect fit, I'd pay her for the time and keep looking.

Right now, however, there was work to do.

I shoved the paper with Vix's number on it into my pocket and made my way to the easel that held my current work in progress. I'd not shown Vix this yet, and for a good reason.

I was stuck.

Picking up a pencil, I made a few alterations to my design and then stepped back for a different perspective. Then I did it again, erasing parts that didn't work and drawing new ones.

I was deep in my work when my phone rang. I recognized my sister London's ringtone, and I automatically picked it up. We both kept odd hours, so we usually texted each other, only calling when something was urgent.

"Hey, London. What's going on?"

"Do you have a minute?" She sounded bothered.

I dropped my pencil and turned away from the easel. "You have good timing. I could use a break. What's up?" London was the baby of the family which meant all of us were protective of her. Or overprotective, if you asked her. I was pretty sure the only reason our parents didn't freak out when she moved to New York after graduating from Boston University was that Maggie and I already lived here.

"You know that play I was telling you and Maggie about? The off-Broadway one? I might have to give it up."

"I remember," I said. "Is someone giving you problems there?"

"No, the play is going well," she said. "I like the role, and the cast is great, but I just got a call from an audition I did for *Pretty Woman* a few months ago. It's a tour all over the country. The girl they originally hired to be the understudy for Vivian got a two-line role in the next Marvel movie and dropped out. They've offered me to be the new understudy."

"And you don't know which to choose."

"I don't mind being an understudy," she said. "And I really like the music from *Pretty Woman*, but the role in this other show is phenomenal. It might not make it to Broadway ever, but she's a character that I'm loving."

"I guess it comes down to what you want more," I said. "The character you love or the opportunity the tour presents."

London was silent for a minute before she sighed.

"You're right. That's what I have to decide. Thanks for letting me talk through things."

"Anytime, sis. Let me know what you're going to do."

"I will."

As I ended the call, I heard the front door open. I figured it was Louis Dubois, my assistant, and manager. Perfect timing.

"Hey, Louis, in here!" Having been with me since I first opened my studio, he was the reason for my success the last few years, working non-stop to get my designs in the right hands to people with deep pockets.

"I just got off the phone with a new supplier from China," he announced as he came over to where I stood, frowning at my design.

I glanced at my watch, surprised at the time, but didn't comment on it. "What did they say?"

"It thrilled them when I told them New York's hottest up-and-comer wants to do business with them." Louis grinned at me, dimples flashing. "You were right about going with this supplier. They confirmed they can handle the amount of silk material you need, and they'll give us a ten percent discount for buying in bulk."

"Perfect," I said with a smile.

When I'd found out my previous supplier was being investigated for labor violations, I knew I had to go somewhere else. Dealing with China could have its challenges. Still, enough research and careful vetting had led me to a new supplier that paid their legally aged employees fair wages and provided safe work conditions. I would've paid more to support a company like that.

"I let them know that if everything goes well, we'll be using them in the future," Louis continued as he dropped onto the couch and put his feet up. "How are things coming here?"

I gestured to the easel. "Better, but still not great. Want a drink? I opened a bottle of Shannon's earlier today."

"I'll take a shot," he said. "I'm going out later, but no harm in having a pre-date drink."

"Rory again, or have you moved on from him?" I asked as I poured Louis and myself a drink.

"Rory," Louis confirmed, his hazel eyes sparkling. "I think he might be the one."

"Well, I'm happy for you," I said as I handed him his glass. "He sounds like a good guy." I raised my glass. "To new partnerships, both business and personal."

We clinked glasses and took a drink before Louis asked, "Speaking of new partnerships, how was your meeting?"

"Good. Baylen's on board with everything." I dug into my pocket and produced the paper with Vix's number. "And I hired a new model."

Louis grabbed the note. "Vixen Teal?" Louis raised an eyebrow. "Seriously?"

I shrugged. "I have siblings named London, Aspen, Blaze, and Fury."

"Good point," Louis said. "What agency is she from?"

"She's not." I gave him a summary of how I'd met her and ignored the disapproval on his face. "Call her to set up a time for measurements and the usual stuff."

"Did you even test her?" he asked. "Is she comfortable undressing in front of people? Can she walk in heels? Stand completely still for hours?"

I finished my drink and avoided answering.

"Fuck Carson, we don't have time to train amateurs. I thought we were going for prime time now. Taking over the fashion world. We agreed that amateur hour was over."

"Look, there's something about her," I said. "I want to give her a chance. See if my instincts are right." I took another sip of whisky. "Call a photographer to get a date for a test shoot, then set things up with her for the week after Maggie's wedding. That'll give me the time to finish the new pieces. Have a standard contract drawn up with exit clauses to protect us if things don't work out."

"All right," he said reluctantly and made a note in his phone. "You're the boss, but I think you're making a mistake. A big one."

FOUR
VIX

"And, of course, there was no reason to be that rude when it was clearly an accident that my boob popped out of my shirt." Monique, one of my other co-workers, was always a lot of fun, though she could be a bit much for anyone who wasn't prepared. "You know how it is for us generously endowed women, right?"

"Ah, yes. Sometimes they escape."

She laughed as she ventured into the Too Much *Irrelevant* Information zone, with more examples of her clothes being inadequate to contain her...endowments.

"There's not much in the stores that girls like us can wear," Monique said. "I mean, the average American woman is a size fourteen or a sixteen. There's only a handful of those sizes here. And nothing above."

"There's actually a designer with a studio close to here that caters to all sizes. Carson McCrae." My stomach twisted as I thought about the call I'd gotten last week from Carson's assistant, Louis, telling me that

Carson still wanted me to model for him. It'd been three weeks since he made me the offer, and I'd worried he had changed his mind, but Louis assured me that Carson had been busy and I'd get a call today or tomorrow with details about when to come in for a test shoot.

"I've heard of him. He is *so* hot but gay, unfortunately." She grabbed my arm, excited. "Don't tell me you know him?"

I shook my head. "Not really. I mean, I met him a few weeks ago. Karen Devereaux sent me to his studio to give him an envelope. You really think he's gay?"

Monique nodded. "Oh honey, he is totally gay. Straight guys do *not* dress that well." She tapped one long acrylic nail on her chin. "You know, I'll bet it was Brietta's portfolio in that envelope. She still thinks she can become a model, that poor delusional girl." She smiled widely. "So, you got to talk to Carson McCrae?"

I grinned, unable to keep my excitement contained any longer. "I did. And he wants me to model for him."

Her jaw dropped. "What! No way! You're pulling my leg, girl."

I laughed. "I swear it's true. His manager contacted me a couple of days ago. I'm going to be modeling a dress and a new line of bras for Carson McCrae at his next fashion show."

Monique squealed, but the sound cut off when a sharp voice came from behind me.

"You're doing *what*?!"

I turned to see Karen Devereaux glaring at me.

Mentally, I cursed, but forced a smile. "Good afternoon, ma'am."

"Answer me." She took a step toward me, her face flushed.

"Mr. McCrae offered me a job modeling some things he's working on," I said. "Of course, I'll work it around my schedule here."

"You bitch!" She raised her hand, and for a moment, I thought she might slap me. Instead, she pointed at me. "You fucked him, didn't you? Gave him a blow job, at the very least. You must have done something to be offered Brietta's job."

I stared at her, unable to believe what was happening. Karen Devereaux could be unreasonable, but this was way beyond that.

"What was it?" she demanded. "What did you do?"

"I did nothing, Mrs. Devereaux," I finally said. "I gave him the envelope, just like you told me to. We talked a bit, and then he asked me if I'd model for him."

Her gaze ran down me and back up again, a sneer on her face. "You really expect me to believe Carson McCrae wants *you* to model for him? With that body? Not likely. Not unless he's doing the 'before' pictures for a weight-loss ad."

At first, I couldn't even think of a response. I didn't give a damn what Karen believed. Yes, she was my boss, but she was also way out of line for workplace behavior.

"You can't speak to me like that." I finally found my voice. "I'm your employee."

"Not anymore, you're not," she snapped. "You're fired."

"For what?" My head spun.

"Insubordination." She made a dismissive gesture. "Not that it matters. It's my store, and I say you're fired. Pack your things and get out."

Less than five minutes later, I was out on the sidewalk in a daze. Of everything I thought might happen today, getting fired from my job was *not* one of them.

I walked on autopilot, my feet taking me to the subway and onto the train that would take me home. I was halfway there before my brain finally processed what had happened. Sure, it was a shock but hardly the most challenging thing I'd faced. Two years ago, I had no job, no place to live, knew no one, and had no practical experience living in the 'real world.' I survived that, and I would do the same now. I just needed to think.

I felt better as I entered the small apartment I shared with Susanna. I had a plan in place. Or, rather, I thought so until I saw the sad expression on my roommate's face.

"What's wrong?" I went to sit next to her.

"Karen called."

My stomach sank, but I kept my voice light. "I'm not worried. You shouldn't be either. I'll get another job right away and be able to pay my share of the rent."

"No, Vix, you don't understand."

A DRESS FOR CURVES

I frowned. "I'll pay the rent on time. I promise."

Susanna shook her head as tears slipped down her cheeks. "She said she'll fire me if I don't kick you out of the apartment."

I blinked, startled. "What? She can't do that."

"That isn't all." Susanna looked at me, her dark eyes full of pain. "I'm undocumented."

"What? I thought you were a born and raised New Yorker."

"My parents came to the US illegally when I was a few weeks old. I was born in Jamaica, and I didn't even know until I started talking about college." She scrubbed her palms against her cheeks. "Only a few people know, but Karen is one of them. She said she'll call ICE on me if I don't make you leave. Not just on me but my parents, too. My siblings."

I couldn't wrap my head around how things had gone so wrong, but I knew one thing for sure. Susanna wasn't going to suffer because Karen Devereaux had a vendetta against me.

I took her hands in mine. "It's going to be okay. I'll pack my things and leave right away. I will not let her hurt you or your family."

"No way," Susanna protested. "I'm not letting her do this. How will she even know if I don't kick you out? Is she going to spy on me?"

I sighed. "She might. She sure is fucked up enough to do that. But, listen, honey, I can find a new job and a new place to stay. This is not the end of the world."

Susanna nodded, and we hugged, her tears wetting my shirt. "I'm so sorry," she cried.

I wiped away her tears. "Don't be. This is entirely my fault. I should never have accepted Carson McCrae's offer."

"Don't say that," she said as she released me. "You did nothing wrong. You deserve this opportunity."

I wasn't sure I agreed, but I didn't want to argue and went to my room, got my suitcase from the closet, and packed my few belongings. I had little. Everything I owned easily fit into that single suitcase.

A minute later, I stepped out of Susanna's apartment for the last time and closed the door behind me.

Just like that, I was unemployed and homeless.

Again.

FIVE
CARSON

I took a step back, finally feeling the satisfaction of getting the design from paper into its final form. Well, more or less final. Now I just needed to see it on Vix to make the adjustments. It surprised me how eager I was to see her wear the dress.

I moved to one of my tables, my head processing the next part, when the sound of the back door opening drew my attention. Very few people had access through that entrance, making me think I knew who it'd be.

"I hoped you'd be here, Carson." The Sussex accent differed from the Scottish brogue I heard from my father, though many Americans probably couldn't tell much of a difference.

"Hey Gigi," I said, sending a smile her way.

Gigi Ainsworth was one of my regular models, though her hailing from England meant I didn't use her often. She was tall and slender, with tawny curls and jade eyes. She was one of those beautiful women I'd spent a lot of time around but felt no real sexual attraction to.

"I have your keys," Gigi said as she came over to me. "Thank you again for letting me stay in your apartment. It's so much nicer than the usual hotel my agency arranges."

"You know you're always welcome to stay here. Anytime." I held out my hand for the keys.

When I purchased my studio, I'd also bought the building behind it, turning the bottom half into a garage and the top into two apartments, though I only used one of them for guests. The other was always full of clothes and excess bolts of fabric that would otherwise clutter up my studio.

"You know, Carson. I always enjoy working with you." She took a step closer to me and reached out to touch the back of my hand. "And I'd like to thank you for your hospitality."

"That's unnecessary." I smiled when I pulled my hand back, not to offend her.

"I know," she said, leaning toward me. "But I'd like to do it, anyway. I'm feeling very grateful."

I repressed a sigh and took a step back. "I'm flattered, Gigi, I really am. But I don't sleep with my models. It's unprofessional."

She stuck out her bottom lip in a mock pout and then laughed. "It's your loss." Then she leaned forward, kissed me on my cheek, and headed back to her luggage.

A DRESS FOR CURVES

I breathed a sigh of relief when the door closed behind her. Models had propositioned me in the past, some of whom were probably honestly attracted to me, but most just wanted the things I could do for them. Turning them down was always the smart move, but it was harder to predict how they would react. Fortunately, Gigi turned out to be cool about it.

The image of Vix popped into my head, and on impulse, I pulled out my phone and called Louis. Instead of answering on the first or second ring, like he usually did, it was the middle of the fifth ring when he finally answered.

"Carson, what's up?" Louis sounded out of breath.

"Are you okay?"

"Fine. Fine. What's going on?"

"I forgot to ask if our new supplier knew when the material would arrive."

"They're supposed to email me tomorrow with the tracking," Louis said. "I'll let you know."

"Thanks. And Vix?" I tried sounding casual. "Have you called her yet to confirm the test shoot?"

"I planned on doing it after I'm done here at the gym."

"The gym?" I didn't disguise my surprise. "Since when do you go to the gym?" Louis was lean, but he never worked out, as far as I knew.

"Since I realized how hot Rory looks in workout clothes. And out of them."

I laughed, shaking my head even though Louis couldn't see me. "I need no more than that, thanks."

"You asked."

"I did," I agreed. "And now I regret it."

I hung up, shaking my head with a smile.

What people would put themselves through for a relationship.

I just didn't have time for that.

SIX
VIX

My head still spun as I carried my lone suitcase down the sidewalk. I needed a place to stay. That had to be my priority. It was September, so shelter wasn't as crucial as it would be in a few months, but I'd no desire to sleep on the street. Tomorrow, I'd scour the city for a new roommate, but until then, I'd stay at a hotel, cheap being the priority. The only one I knew of, without bedbugs and roaches as roommates, was too far to walk.

Since I didn't have the money to waste on a taxi, I turned toward the closest subway entrance, automatically making my way across the platform. Lost in my thoughts, I never noticed the two figures approaching me before it was too late.

I only caught a glimpse of a fist coming toward my face and tried to turn my head. Someone yanked on my purse, spinning me in the opposite direction, and I cried out as the blow connected. As pain radiated through my cheek and jaw, a metallic taste filled my mouth. I stumbled, struggling to keep hold of my purse and suitcase, but they were too strong, and I was outnumbered.

One kicked at me, catching my hip and knocking me sideways. I felt the strap of my purse slide down my arm and tightened my grip on it.

"Let go, bitch!" The man kicked me again as he yanked harder on my purse.

The other grabbed my hair and yanked on it, spinning me before throwing me to the ground. Then I saw a boot go into the air over my hand and did the only thing I could. I let go of my purse and put my arms over my head.

I heard a triumphant yell, a solid thud, and then the train came rushing through. I couldn't stop the tears streaming down my cheeks, but I pressed my lips together, ignoring the pain in my face.

"Miss? Miss, are you all right?" A gentle touch on my arm accompanied the voice.

Slowly, I uncurled, feeling as if hours had passed. An older woman with gray curls and a concerned expression bent over next to me.

"How badly are you hurt?" she asked, a flare of anger in her dark eyes. "My husband's calling 911."

"I...I don't know," I said. "My head hurts." I looked around, although I knew I wouldn't see anything of mine.

"They got away," she confirmed. "And your suitcase…I'm sorry, sweetie, but they threw it onto the tracks. Right in front of the train."

Gone. I slumped in defeat. Everything was gone.

Numbness crept in, and I stared off into space, unsure if I'd responded to anything the woman said. I vaguely registered when the EMTs came, giving them answers to their questions, but nothing more. I ignored the curious stares as they put me into the ambulance and promised myself not to cry until I was finally alone.

Once at the hospital, I put up with the poking and prodding, all the while realizing I didn't have the money to pay for any of this. I never had insurance, but now I didn't even have an income.

At some point, the doctor left, telling me they'd send someone to take me for a CT scan as soon as they could. I nodded and then leaned back in my bed. This was better than a cheap hotel, I supposed.

"Excuse me, Miss?" A man's voice came from the other side of the curtain before he pulled it back. "I'm Horace Newton. I'm a lawyer from MTA." At my blank look, he clarified. "New York City Transportation."

"Oh." I frowned. "I don't understand."

"Have the police been in to talk to you yet?"

I shook my head, then winced as the movement sent a stab of pain through me. "Not yet. I think a nurse said they'd be here soon."

"Excellent." He pulled a chair over to my bed and

sat down. "First, on behalf of the city, let me offer my sympathies regarding your unfortunate incident."

I wasn't sure that was what I'd call it, but I didn't argue.

"To express our concern for your well-being, we'd like to offer to pay your medical bills."

My eyes narrowed. There had to be a catch. Very few people gave anything for free, and governments never did, not even local ones.

"Of course, we'd be doing this with no admission of responsibility on our part and would need you to sign a waiver to that effect." He wiped one chubby hand across his sweating forehead. "Basically, it says that you won't be seeking damages from MTA."

So that was the angle.

"We'll even provide you with a three thousand dollar check to cover the loss of your purse and suitcase." He gave me a condescending smile that made me want to give a less-than-polite response.

The money, however, couldn't have come at a better time. Besides, I wasn't a litigious person. "Okay," I said. "I'll do it."

"Excellent." He glanced over his shoulder as the doctor returned, a nurse at her side. "I'll go get everything drawn up. I just need your full legal name for the paperwork."

"Vixen Teal," I said.

After a momentary pause, he nodded. "All right, Miss Teal. I'll be back soon."

As he left, the doctor said, "We're ready to take you

for the CT scan. No matter how that comes back, I'd like to keep you overnight for observation. You took a pretty good hit to the head. We want to make sure there's no concussion."

Considering my options were limited at the moment, and MTA was footing this bill, the answer was simple.

"Whatever you think is best, doc." I'd figure the rest out later.

SEVEN
CARSON

I smiled at the picture on my screen, even though I'd seen it already. The dress I'd designed was gorgeous, but that wasn't the reason I kept looking at it. It was the smile on my little sister's face that captured my attention. Maggie had been through a rough year—and a couple before that, as I'd only recently learned—but her marriage to Drake Mac Gilleain was the beginning of something new and wonderful for her. He was a good man, and she deserved every happiness.

Still, even my pleasant memories of the past weekend couldn't stop me from impatiently checking the clock every few minutes, wondering what was keeping Louis. I never paid much attention to his comings and goings, but today was different, and I wasn't sure I liked the reason for it.

"Good morning," Louis called out as he came in. "I brought coffee."

About goddamn time.

"Thanks." I accepted the cup and sipped it without really tasting it. "You didn't get back to me last night about Vix. I'd like to get to her this week."

Louis frowned, a strange expression on him. "Yeah, that's weird. I haven't been able to get in touch with her. I called her several times yesterday, but it kept going straight to voicemail."

"You tried this morning?"

"I have," he said. "And the same."

It was my turn to frown. "Keep trying."

"Don't worry, buddy. I will." He walked over to the dress I'd designed for Vix. "It's lovely. This is your best in a long time. I'm still not sure about her, though. I just hope it looks as good on her as it does here."

"It will," I promised as I turned myself back to a few final touches on Baylen's bra.

It wasn't easy to focus on the work, and as time grew closer to noon, my impatience got the better of me.

Was she blowing me off? That would be new. If Vix wouldn't answer Louis's calls, perhaps she needed a face-to-face meeting. I decided I could use a walk and told Louis as much. I didn't walk the entire way from lower Manhattan, though. After a couple of blocks, I waved down a cab and had it take me to my least favorite place.

Soie et Velours.

As I entered the shop, I lost hope that the Devereaux women wouldn't be there. The first person to greet me was none other than the worse of the two, Karen.

"Carson! How wonderful to see you!" She gave me a broad smile and fluttered her eyelashes at me.

Fluttered. Her. Eyelashes.

"Are you here to talk to Brietta?"

"Brietta?"

"Yes." Karen Devereaux moved until she was nearly in my personal space. "She'll be the perfect face for your new line. She has a perfect model's body, after all."

Brietta. Right. The headshots I'd thrown away without even looking at them.

"No, actually. I'm not here to talk to Brietta...um... yet." I needed Karen to let me talk to Vix. "I haven't made a final decision."

"Oh." Her smile faded.

"But I would like to speak to one of your employees." I forced a smile. "Vixen Teal."

Karen Devereaux's expression turned to stone. "Why do you want to see her?"

"I just have a few things I need to discuss."

"Well, she's not here." Karen pursed her lips.

"Is she not working today?" I had assumed that was why she didn't answer her phone this morning.

"I have no idea what she's doing," Karen said. "I caught her stealing and fired her."

My eyebrows shot up. "Stealing. Really?"

"She's lucky I didn't call the cops."

"Mrs. Devereaux," someone called from the back of the store. "I have a call for you."

"I'm sorry, Carson. People just can't leave me alone. I look forward to seeing you again when you come to talk to Brietta about details for your next line." Karen Devereaux sauntered away.

Dammit. I sighed. What now?

I was halfway to the door when a young woman with gorgeous dark skin came up beside me, a strange expression on her face.

"You're looking for Vix?"

"I am." Judging by how she kept glancing back to where Devereaux was talking on the phone, I assumed she worked here. "Do you know where she is?"

"Meet me outside in five minutes."

I stared at the woman as she hurried away but didn't linger. I continued on my way. Once outside, I found a spot out of sight from the doors and waited. Five minutes later, almost to the second, the doors opened, and the same woman came out.

"I'm Carson McCrae," I said, holding out a hand. "Fashion designer."

"I know who you are." Now that she was out of the shop, she seemed more sure of herself. "Don't believe that witch for a second. Vix wasn't stealing."

"Oh, I didn't think she would."

She gave me a searching look and then nodded. "I'm Susanna. Vix's friend and, until yesterday, roommate."

"Until yesterday?" That didn't sound good.

A DRESS FOR CURVES

Susanna looked distressed. "When Karen Devereaux heard you offered Vix a modeling job, she fired her immediately and forced me to kick Vix out of our apartment. She said I'd be out of a job too if I didn't."

I bit back the unpleasant things I wanted to say about Karen Devereaux.

"Vix packed her things and left. I haven't heard from her since."

"Did you really expect to hear from her after kicking her out like that?" I winced at my harsh tone. "I'm sorry."

Susanna shook her head. "No, I get it. Vix is my friend, but Mrs. Devereaux blackmailed me into doing it. Vix understood, though. She wasn't angry with me."

I rubbed the back of my neck. "Would you mind doing me a favor? I know this might be weird, but can you call her? I need to know if she's not answering my assistant because she no longer wants to model for me or if something's wrong."

"Of course." She pulled her phone out of her pocket and tapped the screen. It only took a moment before she frowned. "Straight to voicemail. She never sends it straight to voicemail."

"Maybe the phone's off, or her battery died?" Both completely reasonable explanations.

Susanna shook her head. "Vix never lets her phone die, and she never turns it off. Silence it, yes, but not off. Ever. Not in the two years since I've known her." Susanna glanced behind her. "I have to get back."

I nodded as she left, but my mind was elsewhere. Specifically, it was with Vix. Something just didn't sit right with me about all of this.

I had to find her sooner rather than later. Time could be of the essence. I reached inside my pocket for my phone and started making calls.

EIGHT
VIX

Not only did I get the medical all-clear, which was good, but also a three-thousand-dollar check to cash, which was even better. What I didn't have, however, was a place to stay.

I'll think of something. I always do.

All those thoughts flew out of my head as soon as I stepped out of the hospital. "Carson? I mean, Mr. McCrae."

"Carson, please," he said with a smile that didn't quite reach his eyes.

Why was he here?

"How did you find me?"

"I made a few calls." He took a step toward me.

"Why?"

"Because you weren't answering Louis's calls, and I was worried." He reached out to brush the back of his finger over my swollen cheek. "Who did this to you?"

I swallowed hard and pushed away the heat that

came from his touch. "Looks like my modeling career is over before it started," I quipped.

"Not at all." He gave me a soft smile. "We have some time. And I have a genius make-up artist."

Suddenly, my stomach growled.

"You must be starving. Let me take you to lunch," he said. "We can discuss the next step. If you still want to model for me, that is."

I was honestly too exhausted to think much and just accepted. "Thank you."

"My car's this way," he said. "Do you need help?"

I shook my head. "I've got some bruises, but it looks worse than it is."

We made our way to his car and rode in silence to a small diner I recognized as down the street from his studio. It wasn't until we were both settled into a corner booth that he asked the question I knew was coming.

"What happened?" A flash of anger crossed his face as he looked at the bruise again. "Your friend Susanna told me that you were fired and then the Devereaux bitch blackmailed her into kicking you out, but how did you go from that to a hospital?"

"You talked to Susanna?"

"I went to the boutique to find you, and she was there. We tried calling you, but you didn't pick up."

"I don't have a phone anymore." I frowned as I thought of what it would take to replace everything I'd lost. The money from the MTA would help with the phone, at least. "That's part of the story of how I ended up in the hospital."

The server arrived and set our food in front of us. The hunger gnawing at my stomach took precedence.

"What happened yesterday? Getting fired and kicked out of your apartment didn't put you in the hospital or take your phone."

"No," I said wryly. "That would be the two masked men who mugged me on the subway platform, stole my purse, and threw my suitcase in front of the train."

"You're not joking?" The surprise then anger that blazed on Carson's face shocked me. "What will you do now?" He reached toward me, then seemed to think better of it.

"I'll be alright." I gave him the best smile I could muster. "I actually spoke with someone from the MTA yesterday. They're taking care of my medical bills, and they gave me a check. Once I cash it, I have enough to tide me over until I get a new job."

"I still want you to model for me," Carson said. "We can do a test shoot tomorrow afternoon if you're up for it. You'll get paid for your time, of course."

"Tomorrow? Even with this?" I gestured to my cheek.

"It's just a test shoot," Carson said. "It'll just be me, my assistant, Louis, and a photographer. But if you're self-conscious about it–"

"No, I don't mind," I blurted out. "Thank you. I'm really grateful for the opportunity. And it'll help a lot to have that income while I'm hunting for a new job. I love the city, but it's not a cheap place to live."

"It's not," he agreed.

I excused myself to use the restroom, and when I came back, Carson had taken care of the bill and was ready to go.

"I'll drop you off wherever you're staying," he said.

"That's all right," I said. "I'll be getting a room at a hotel, and since I'll need to cash this check first...." I frowned as something occurred to me. "Dammit. My ID. It was in my purse, and I don't think I can get a hotel room without it."

"Don't you have any family?"

"Not around here." I shook my head, hoping he wouldn't ask more questions regarding my origins. "Don't worry about me. I'll figure something out."

"I will not let you wander off into the city without a place to stay," Carson said. "You can stay in my apartment." My eyes went wide, and he flushed. "No, no. That's not what I meant. I have a spare apartment behind my studio. I regularly let guests and out-of-town models stay there. It needs to be cleaned up," he continued, "since Gigi just left yesterday. I can have that taken care of right away. You can stay there until you find a permanent place."

I gave him a tight smile. "I doubt your girlfriend would want me staying there."

"Gigi's not my girlfriend," Carson said. "She's a model."

"Ah."

A DRESS FOR CURVES

"I never sleep with my models," he continued. "I'd make the same offer to anyone in your situation. I *have* made this offer to plenty of other people I have never slept with."

Sincerity rang in every word, and I believed him. "Okay," I said. "Thank you. But I insist on paying rent, so there's no question about it being a business arrangement."

He nodded. "Of course. We'll work something out. How does that sound?"

"Perfect." I stuck out my hand. "Deal?"

Smiling, he took my hand. I nearly gasped at the shock that went through me the minute we touched. Something flickered in his eyes, making me think he felt it too, but he simply shook my hand and released it.

"I'll tell my housekeeper to get started. She won't have the apartment ready until later this afternoon."

"That's not a problem. I need to run a few errands. Cash the check. Get a new phone. Some clothes."

He nodded. "Let me know if you need any help with that? I got a couple of hours."

I appreciated the fact that he asked and remembered something. "If I could ask one more favor?"

"Of course."

"Since they stole my wallet, I don't have my ID. I really hate to wait several days for the check to clear. Could I sign the check over to you, and you can cash it for me?"

"Of course. I'm happy to help," he said. "Why

don't we go to my bank now? We can cash the check there."

Half an hour later, we walked out of the bank with three thousand dollars in my pocket. Carson held out a business card. "Be careful. Don't let people see you have that much money on you. My number is on the card. When you get your phone, put it in. You can always call me if you need anything. I'll see you tonight."

"Thank you." Those two words hardly seemed enough for everything Carson had done for me, but they would have to do for now.

I turned my attention to all the things I needed to get done.

NINE
CARSON

As I opened the door for Vix and stepped aside to let her pass, I was strangely nervous, wanting her to like it. I'd even told my housekeeper to get some flowers for the place, something I never did for anyone else. I convinced myself it was because she'd been through a trauma.

"This place is amazing."

The look on her face as she took in the surroundings warmed me. It was the larger of the two apartments at a little over a thousand square feet. I'd put in top-of-the-line appliances and the best furniture, wanting it to look like a place someone could feel more at home than they would in a hotel.

"Gigi left some unopened food, so please help yourself to anything." I didn't add that I'd also told my housekeeper to pick up a few essentials besides the flowers. "There are two bedrooms, one with an attached bathroom. There's also a half-bath, all down that hall."

"I think this is twice the size of the apartment I shared with Susanna." Vix set down the bags she'd insisted on carrying up herself. "This is incredible."

"Well, there is one other thing I'd like to show you before I go back to the studio."

"There's more?"

"This way." I led her back out into the small hallway and unlocked the other door. "Technically, this is also an apartment, but I use it as storage space, especially when I'm working on a show and need more room downstairs."

I flipped on the light and smiled when I heard her gasp.

"You're welcome to borrow anything you see." I gestured to the giant clothing rack to the left. "The smallest sizes start there and increase as you go. Not everything in here is practical, but you can never tell what you'll need, right? There are some shoes at the back, too."

"This is too much." Vix surprised me by grabbing my hand. "I mean it, Carson. It's just too much."

I squeezed her hand. "I'm glad to help you get back on your feet." After a moment, I cleared my throat and took a step back, releasing her hand. I held out the keys. "We can sign a month-to-month lease agreement tomorrow with the modeling contract."

Before I could come up with a reason to stick around, I made my way back to my studio. I had a bunch of stuff to do, starting with figuring out something to eat. I ordered my usual favorites from the Chinese place, and while I waited for the delivery guy, my mind kept returning to the woman above the garage. To the bruise on her face and the ones I couldn't see.

A surge of anger went through me, and I wondered if the police had made any progress in finding the men who'd mugged her. I doubted she'd ever get any of her things back, but those guys had to be taken off the streets. Luckily, this time nobody got killed, but who could say they wouldn't escalate next time?

My mind flashed back to my sister, Maggie, and the violence her ex had committed against her. I had to make sure what happened to Vix didn't get lost on some overworked detective's desk. Fortunately, I still had the number of the detective who'd worked with Maggie, and I called him.

"Detective Kozuch?"

"Speaking."

"This is Carson McCrae. I don't know if you remember me—"

"Of course, Mr. McCrae. Is your sister okay?"

"Yes. She's well," I said. "I'm actually calling about something else."

"Go on."

I explained everything Vix shared with me and asked, "Have you heard anything about it?"

"I haven't, but let me make some calls, and I'll get back to you."

"Thank you," I said.

"No problem. Send my congratulations to Mr. and Mrs. Mac Gilleain, will you?"

"Sure thing," I promised.

My food arrived, and afterward, I prepared for tomorrow's shoot. That was one of the things that gave me an edge. Talent was important, of course, but people often underestimated good planning.

Except I couldn't concentrate.

As I laid out color swatches to test against Vix tomorrow, I kept picturing her lying on a bed, with just those tiny pieces of cloth draped across her body. Not covering anything. Teasing and tempting.

I muttered a curse and reached down to adjust myself.

Focus.

I turned to the dress I'd designed with Vix in mind. Next to it were the matching bra and panty set I'd also created for her. Baylen's bra design, featuring an innovative support system, could be adapted for any body type, but it worked exceptionally well for a woman with curves. A woman just like Vix. I already had a few models lined up for my show, and they'd all be wearing their versions of it, but I'd been anticipating this moment since the beginning. To finally see the bra on the perfect body type.

It had nothing to do with how insanely hot Vix was or how she'd look in those bits of lace and silk.

"Dammit." I sighed. This wasn't working. It didn't help that I knew Vix could be upstairs right now, changing into one of my designs. I could think of a dozen outfits I'd like to see her in.

And then get her out of them.

My cock was almost painfully hard, and I didn't see that changing soon with no help.

I leaned back in my seat, hating myself a bit, as I closed my eyes and undid my pants.

I groaned the moment my fingers closed around my shaft. It wouldn't take much to get me off. I moved my closed hand up and down at a quick pace as I jacked off. Behind my eyelids danced images of Vix, in and out of my designs. In my bed. Bent over the couch. Sitting on the table.

On her knees.

"Fuck!" I groaned as I stepped up the pace. Squeezing my fist harder around my shaft, I came with an explosion, the pleasure blanking out my mind.

As I stepped into the bathroom to clean up, I told myself that I had done nothing wrong. I wasn't pursuing Vix, and I would be entirely professional whenever she modeled for me. Maybe after the show was over, and she no longer worked for me, I'd see if there could be something between us.

Now, I had to get back to work.

TEN
VIX

When I first arrived in Manhattan, I met Susanna almost immediately, and she referred me to her employer, Karen Devereaux, who needed a new salesperson. Karen had hired me on the spot, so I never had to do any of...*this*.

Going from store to store, looking for "Help Wanted" signs, and filling out a dozen applications was...tiring. But, it shouldn't take long. I was living in New York City, and opportunities were everywhere.

As planned, I headed back to the studio a little before noon. My nerves, which I had ignored all day, now demanded attention. Carson had assured me that a test shoot was nothing to be anxious about, but he wasn't the one about to do something completely crazy. Like thinking I could be a model.

I took pride in being a free-spirited woman but never had I done anything remotely close to this.

When I entered the studio, Carson and a man I

assumed was Louis were waiting. The latter was on the phone, and I recognized his voice from our conversations. He gave me a wave of acknowledgment but kept on with his phone call.

Carson appeared engrossed in something he was working on, but when he looked up, his eyes widened.

"Nice dress."

"Thanks. It's one of yours." I smiled as I smoothed down the sundress I'd found last night. Perfect for a warm September day.

"It looks good on you." He left whatever he was working on and came toward me. The look in his eyes as he studied me could have been professional, seeing how the clothes he had made fit me, but I saw a spark of heat in them that made my heart skip a beat.

"That was Jon on the phone," Louis said as he interrupted us. "The photographer I hired for today."

"Is he okay?" Carson said, all business again. "He was supposed to be here fifteen minutes ago."

"He's stuck in traffic," Louis said. "Still a few minutes out."

Carson frowned, forehead furrowing as he thought. "All right. Let's get started, anyway. Louis, this is Vix. Vix, this is Louis."

"Nice to put a face to the voice," I said to Louis as I smiled.

"Louis, keep an eye out for Jon and have him set up in the usual space. I'll get started on Vix's measurements and get her changed."

A DRESS FOR CURVES

I pressed my damp palms against my sides and nodded. "What do you need me to do?"

"Undress." I must've looked startled because Carson's expression softened. "Sorry. I forgot you've never done this before. I need to get some measurements, and while I can do that with you clothed, it's easier if you're in your underwear."

"Right." I nodded as if it was something I'd merely forgotten rather than didn't know.

I could do this.

"Hey." Carson took my hand. "You can change your mind if you're not comfortable. I know not everyone is okay with being around a bunch of strangers wearing nothing but your underwear."

I shook my head. "No, it's not that. I just realized that I'm a little in over my head. I've done nothing like this before."

He squeezed my hand before releasing it. "I'll take you through it all, step by step, but only if you still want to do it."

"I do." I reached for the dress's side zipper and pulled it down.

My underwear was simple, especially compared to some of the pieces Carson had designed, but they were not that revealing. Not that it would have mattered to me. I'd grown up in a free-spirited place without the body and sex-shaming prevalent in society, so being completely nude didn't bother me.

"Stand there, please," Carson said, barely glancing

at me as he motioned to a small platform. "Leave your shoes on for the moment."

I did as he asked, trying to keep my face blank while he wrapped his tape measure around my waist. The brush of his fingers sent goosebumps racing across my skin, and I flushed, hoping he wouldn't notice my body's reaction. If he did, he never commented on it. With laser focus, he took various measurements, speaking to me only when he needed me to move.

I relaxed as the time passed, but it did nothing to stop the jolts of electricity every time he touched me. I couldn't help wondering if he felt them too, but absolutely nothing on his face betrayed his thoughts. He was a complete professional, even if a small part of me wished he wasn't. Not seriously, of course, but I couldn't deny I was attracted to him.

"All right," he said finally, taking a step back. "None of your measurements surprised me, so there shouldn't be much in the way of adjustments needed."

"Do you do new measurements each time?" I asked as I stepped off the platform.

"Not usually, no." He walked over to a rack and took something off. "If the bra and underwear fit fine, put on the dress. I'll make any adjustments to that, and hopefully, Jon will be ready by then. We'll do shots of you in the dress and then you in the bra and underwear since the bra will also be part of my show."

I nodded and took the clothes into the dressing room. The bra and panties were sexier than mine, but not so much that they weren't practical, a formidable combination, especially for women built like me. I took a moment to admire myself in the mirror before slipping into the dress.

"Whoa," I whispered when I saw my reflection. This was the dress I'd seen Carson sketching when I first met him, and it was even more beautiful in real life. Soft silk clung to my curves, the deep purple suiting my coloring perfectly. I almost felt like I was disrespecting it when I put on my sensible shoes to go back into the main room.

"All right, Vix, back onto...." Carson's voice trailed off as he raised his head and saw me. His mouth hung open for a few seconds before he seemed to catch himself and snapped it shut. He pointed to the platform.

I supposed that answered the questions I had about how I looked. Pleased, I carefully stepped up onto the platform and then changed into the pair of heels Carson handed me.

It was harder than I imagined, staying completely still while Carson's hand moved over my body, always professional even when touching me in some pretty intimate places. I wondered if it would be different with another designer. If I'd feel awkward or if it'd be easier.

"How are your feet doing?" Carson asked.

"A little sore," I admitted. "I didn't realize there'd be so much standing."

"Many people don't," he said. "Especially not this

part. People don't think about how physically demanding it all is."

"Well, even if this is the only time I do this, I'll never look at a billboard or magazine the same way again."

"How comfortable is the dress?" he asked, taking a step back to get a better look. "Can you move without feeling like you're going to rip it?"

Tentatively, I moved my arms, my muscles stiff from being in the same position. Moved my legs, my hips. Bent and twisted, doing nothing fast in case something was too tight.

"I wouldn't want to run a marathon in it, but I can move," I said finally.

"Excellent." He turned and called across the room. "Jon, are you ready?"

"I am," the answer came back immediately.

"Ready for the next step?" Carson held out a hand.

I nodded as I took his hand and let him help me down from the platform. I had to concentrate enough on walking that I barely noticed when he let me go.

Barely.

"Vix, this is Jon Rankin," Carson said.

"Hi." A man thin enough to be called skinny held out one bony hand.

"Hello, Mr. Rankin." I shook his hand. "Just tell me what to do."

"Let's get you under these lights and start there," Jon said with a friendly smile.

A DRESS FOR CURVES

I nodded and made my way over to the spot he showed.

"She looks phenomenal," Louis said.

"She does," Carson agreed. "The dress isn't perfect, though. Not yet. But it'll do for a test."

And with that, he turned things over to Jon. I couldn't see much in the shadows, so I hardly noticed Carson, but every so often, as I was turned and posed, I felt the weight of a gaze on me that felt different from the others. Hotter. Sharper.

However, by the time the photographer took his last snapshot, people watching me was the furthest thing from my mind. A light sheen of sweat coated my skin, and my muscles ached. My feet had gone numb an hour ago, and I had a feeling that as soon as I took these shoes off, I wouldn't be able to get them back on. At least I didn't have far to go to a shower and comfy pajamas.

"Great job, Ms. Teal," Jon said. "I wouldn't have guessed this was your first time."

"Really? I'm so relieved to hear that." Spots danced in front of my eyes when the lights went off, and when they adjusted, I saw Louis waiting nearby.

"You can change back into your regular clothes," Louis said. "Just leave those in the dressing room, and I'll take care of them."

I nodded, trying not to be too obvious as I looked around the room.

"He's drawing out some changes," Louis answered my unasked question.

"Oh, okay. I wasn't sure if Carson wanted to talk to me before I left."

"When he's working, nothing gets through to him," Louis said with a laugh. "He'll probably be here past midnight and not realize he's alone."

"Am I really that bad?" Carson suddenly appeared behind him. Even though he was speaking to Louis, his eyes found me. "You were great, Vix. Better than I imagined."

"Thank you." I flushed, and it wasn't from the heat of the lights.

"Louis, let's get that contract handled. Will you?"

ELEVEN
CARSON

Done.

I stepped back from the dress and made a slow circle around it, critiquing every inch and stitch. Then I looked at the pictures of Vix that Jon emailed. I knew that I'd been right about recruiting her.

Honestly, it would've taken an awful test shoot not to hire her. She possessed all the qualities I could want in a model to fulfill my vision of an all-types-of-women clothing line. That long, white-blonde hair. Unique light violet eyes that I didn't think I'd ever seen anywhere else.

And that body.

Damn.

My phone rang, stopping me in my tracks before I could venture into dangerous territory.

"Hello?"

"Carson, it's Baylen."

"Great timing. I got a few updates for you."

"Wonderful," Baylen said. "Are you free for a couple of hours? Harlee and I just arrived in town. We took a layover on our way back to Scotland from California. She wants to go shopping, but I was hoping you could get me out of it. Do you have time to meet me for a drink and catch me up on everything?"

"Absolutely," I said. "Where are you now?"

"At The Plaza. Do you want to meet here or somewhere else?"

I thought for a moment and then said, "Caledonia Bar on Park Avenue, in say, forty minutes?"

"Perfect. And thanks for getting me out of shopping."

I laughed as I hung up. I was tempted to ask Vix if she could join us, and if Harlee had been going, I might have, but it'd be awkward for Vix to be at a bar with two men she hardly knew.

Not wanting to limit my drinks, I called for a car and arrived at the bar just as Baylen walked in. A minute later, the two of us were perched on stools at the far end, waiting for the bartender to bring us our glasses of—what else?—Shannon's Whisky.

"I'm assuming you brought that to show me some designs?" Baylen gestured toward the laptop I'd set on the bar.

"And pictures," I said, pulling up the files. "I did a test shoot with Vix today."

"Vix?"

"The young woman you and Harlee met when you were here last time," I reminded him.

"The hot blonde?" I shot him a glare, and he laughed. "Just a general observation. I'm quite happy with my own blonde."

"And she'd probably kick your ass if she heard you calling another woman hot," I said.

"She made a similar comment about you, so I think I'd be fine." Baylen grinned. "Harlee is amazing."

"You sound like my brother when he talks about Lumen," I said. "Or, honestly, Brody and Eoin and the Mercier sisters. You've all got it bad."

"What about you?" Baylen asked. "Anyone you've taken a fancy to?"

"I've got a bit too much on my plate right now for romance," I said. "Here."

Baylen fell silent as he went through the designs I'd sketched out. Finally, he leaned back. "Damn. Those are fantastic. I love the changes."

"Thank you," I said. "Now, I have Vix in a dress I designed, wearing your bra underneath. She's the one I want modeling the bra, too."

Baylen let out a whistle as I showed him the pictures of Vix. "I knew she was hot, but that's...." He made a gesture to say that he couldn't find the words.

I knew how he felt.

"She's perfect," I said. When Baylen glanced at me, I clarified. "For the clothing line. I don't get involved with my models."

Baylen nodded. "Aye. I can see how that could get complicated."

"I'm going to have her be the feature model for my

designs in my next show, but I want you to give me the okay before I officially make her the face of the bra."

"Oh, man. You have my blessing," Baylen said. He took a long drink of his whisky. "Now, I'm curious. If you don't date your models, where *do* you find your dates?"

I chuckled. "At the moment, work is my only relationship. I don't mind, though. I love what I do."

That was the truth. I loved my work, but as I closed Vix's images on my screen, I couldn't help wondering if maybe there would be time for something more down the road.

TWELVE
VIX

I WAS WORRIED SOMETHING WAS WRONG WITH ME. The last three days, I'd turned in applications to at least a dozen boutiques looking to hire, and I hadn't gotten a single call back.

I didn't understand it. The last time I looked for a job, I got hired with no credentials. Now, I had two years of work experience, and nobody wanted me. It made no sense.

I couldn't let the frustration show on my face. Walking from place to place, in and out of the oppressive heat, had left me drooping. Not ideal for a first impression, so I plastered on my best smile as I opened the door to yet another store, this one selling high-end lingerie with prices I could never hope to afford.

"Hi," I said, approaching the saleswoman. "I noticed the sign in the window saying that you're hiring. Can I get an application?"

The smile she returned was pleasant, and hope

flourished that this time would be different. She dug around in a drawer for a moment and handed me a piece of paper. "Here you go."

"Is it okay if I fill it out here?" I asked.

"Sure." She pointed to a space tucked in the corner. "Right over there."

"Thanks." I smiled and took the pen she offered before moving to the spot.

I was halfway through the paperwork when familiar voices made me look up. Karen and Brietta Devereaux glared at me like I was something they needed to scrape off their shoes.

"I hope you're not applying for a job here," Karen Devereaux said, her voice booming. "Because no one wants to work with a thief."

My jaw dropped, shock radiating through me. "I'm no thief."

"You really shouldn't waste everyone's time," Brietta said, patting down her hair. "They've all called your previous employer, my mom, who's informing them what a lousy employee you were and how things mysteriously disappeared from the store every time you were working."

"What?" The word came out as a whisper.

"Did you think Mom was going to vouch for you?" Brietta laughed. "No, everyone who has called knows that you're lazy and a thief."

"Not to mention your dreadful appearance. How can you bring yourself to wear such a horrible-looking outfit?" Karen Devereaux gave me a withering, disapproving look.

Pieces of the puzzle clicked into place as I realized why nobody had called back. Of course, people called my most recent employer, and Karen Devereaux would lie to harm me. It tempted me to tell her my outfit she found so dreadful was a Carson McCrae design, but I held back. No need to involve Carson any further with Karen Devereaux.

"Let me give you some good advice," Karen continued, dark eyes glittering with malice. "Move away. Leave the city. There's nothing left for you here. Nobody in their right mind will ever hire you."

Karen Devereaux glanced at the woman behind the counter, who'd been watching the exchange without saying a word. "I think we're done here, Brietta. We still have shopping to do."

I watched the pair walk away and then I looked at the saleswoman. The stricken expression on her face told me she was torn, but I wouldn't put her in a position where she'd have to take sides.

I folded up the paper and slid it across the counter toward her with a small smile. "Could you throw that away for me? I won't be applying today."

Now, what was I going to do?

THIRTEEN
CARSON

"Dammit."

I stuck my finger in my mouth to stop blood from dripping on the fabric. I moved to the drawer where I kept the band-aids and pulled one out. I wanted to finish pinning this bit before I stopped for the day. Now that I had Baylen's approval for Vix to be the model for his bra, I'd started working on more designs. I'd barely slept in the last few days, but it was worth it.

A few minutes later, I slid the last pin into place and took a step back to get a better look at the dress taking shape. I could easily imagine it on my models. Specifically, in this case, Vix.

A jolt of desire hit me, and I relished it for a moment before scolding myself.

Be professional, Carson.

Vix kept popping into my thoughts regularly now and I felt like a testosterone-laden teenager who couldn't control his cock.

I sighed as I glanced toward the front door, hoping she might come through here on her way back to the apartment. Though I hadn't spoken to her today, I suspected she'd been out job hunting.

My phone interrupted my thoughts.

"Carson McCrae."

"It's Detective Kozuch." I recognized his voice.

"Any news, detective?"

"Yes, I got an update, Mr. McCrae. They found surveillance video of the assault, and we now have a clean screenshot of their faces. It'll just be a matter of days before they are caught."

"Excellent. Thank you, detective, and please let me know when you have caught the bastards."

I heard the front door open and ended the call. A smile broke across my face when I saw Vix's familiar form.

"Hey, glad you're here. I just finished another dress for the show. Do you have time tomorrow for a fitting?" I asked before I got a good look at her expression, and now I wished I'd waited.

"Sure." Her smile was tired and didn't reach her eyes.

"Any time before noon works," I said. "It should only take an hour."

"All right. I can come around ten." She turned to go to the stairs, her entire body looking drained.

"Are you all right?" So much for keeping it all business.

She sighed, a sad, lonely sound, and turned back

toward me. "I suppose you'll hear it, eventually."

"Hear what?"

"Karen Devereaux has essentially blackballed me from anything to do with fashion, including working at any clothing store in the city."

I frowned. "I don't know what Karen Deveraux has told you, but she doesn't have that sort of clout in the industry."

"I found out why I haven't gotten a single call back on my applications. All the stores contacted Karen Devereaux, my previous employer, who's been lying about what happened. I'll have to look for work outside the fashion industry."

Anger toward Karen Devereaux filled me. I hated that I became the reason for Karen's vendetta against Vix, simply because I'd preferred Vix to her daughter as my new model.

An idea popped into my head. "Or...you could give my name as your most recent employer and let me be your reference."

"You?"

I wished she didn't sound so shocked. "Yes, me."

"You've done so much to help me already. Are you sure?"

I took a step toward her. "You don't deserve to have your reputation destroyed like that. You're a good person, Vix."

"Thank you." Her cheeks were pink. "But I can't ask you to do that."

"You're not asking me," I said. "I'm offering."

"But I don't exactly work for you..." she said. "I mean, I technically do, but there's a big difference between a little modeling and full-time employment."

"No one needs to know that. I would give you an honest and glowing recommendation." I couldn't stop myself from moving closer to her.

Damn.

She smelled fantastic.

"You're hard-working, compassionate, and good with people. Any employer would be lucky to have you."

"Those are kind words." Her voice was soft as her eyes met mine. "But I don't want people to think badly of you because of me."

I shook my head. "It won't go like that. People will believe me over Karen Devereaux, trust me."

She surprised me by taking my hand and giving it a squeeze. "Thank you. That means a lot."

I could've walked away right then. Taken the memory of her hand in mine back to my place and spent some quality time imagining what it would feel like to have those fingers wrapped around my cock.

Instead, I pulled her toward me. I caught a glimpse of surprise in the seconds before our mouths collided. Instant heat and electricity shot through me, obliterating all coherent thought.

What I'd meant to be a quick kiss changed into much more when Vix leaned into me. She made a soft noise in the back of her throat as I traced her bottom lip with the tip of my tongue, then opened her mouth, inviting me to explore. I wrapped my arms around her waist, hauling her up against my body. Soft curves pressed against the hard parts of me—including parts that were getting harder by the second—and I walked us backward until her back was against the wall.

As her tongue tangled with mine, I tugged her hair out of its twist and buried my fingers in it. In the general process of measuring and fitting, I brushed against her hair from time to time, but nothing could have prepared me for the reality. The strands slipped through my fingers like pure silk, and my body tightened at the thought of what that would feel like spilling over my bare skin.

Her hands moved down my back, then up under my shirt. A shiver went through me as her fingernails raked up my spine. I pressed my thigh between her legs and rocked against her, drawing out the sexiest moan I'd ever heard. I swallowed the sound and scraped my teeth over her bottom lip, barely holding back the urge to bite down.

I wanted to taste her. Pull down the front of her dress and bra, take that sensitive flesh into my mouth, and suck until it was tight. Worry at it with my teeth. I wanted to go to my knees and put her legs over my shoulders, bury my face between her thighs. Lick every inch of her.

Take her hard and fast right here against the wall in the garage–

I suddenly remembered my firm rule of never sleeping with a model.

I cursed and pulled back.

I couldn't let it happen.

She was my newest model. She was living in my spare apartment. There were so many reasons this couldn't happen. Not even as a casual fling.

"I'm sorry." My voice was hoarse.

I turned away, running my hands through my hair. I couldn't look at Vix, couldn't see if her lips were swollen from my kisses, her hair mussed. I didn't want to know if she was flushed, as aroused as I was.

"This was a mistake. I'm sorry." I walked away without looking back and hoped she'd forget all about it.

Whether I wanted her to forget that I kissed her or forget that I stopped, I didn't know.

FOURTEEN
VIX

It was all my fault.

I shouldn't have grabbed Carson's hand yesterday. Touching him had been a bad idea. And I'd made it worse by kissing him back.

But his kiss...

Damn.

Yes, I grew up in a sexually open environment where no one was shamed for their desires. But holy moly, I'd never been kissed like that before.

Fireworks.

That's what it felt like. Lights and colors exploding inside me. The percussion that came with each detonation had made my heart stutter.

I'd wilted when he'd pulled back and told me it was a mistake, although I knew he was right. But that didn't ease the ache that was left behind.

The dress fitting this morning hadn't made it any easier. Feeling Carson's hands all over me as he adjusted the fabric was almost too much. I'd done my best to avoid eye contact, and every time his hand brushed my bare skin, I pretended it didn't make me hot and bothered.

Finally, after an hour of intense heat and temptation, I breathed a sigh of relief when we were done. I returned to the apartment to make myself a light lunch before spending the afternoon planning my next step while I looked for job openings online. With Carson's offer to use him as my work reference, my chances of finding a new job had improved considerably.

But it was hard to concentrate. My mind kept wandering to the kiss, so I was grateful when my phone rang.

I glanced at the caller id. It was Susanna.

"What's up?" I asked, hoping my cheerful tone showed I didn't blame her one bit for what had happened.

"Hey, are you free tonight? I just got on the list for the opening of DIVA. It's a plus-one if you're game."

"No way. How did you manage that?"

DIVA was the most talked-about nightclub for the creative crowd, and it hadn't even opened yet. Anyone who was anyone—or who wanted to *be* anyone—wanted on the guest list. We'd heard Brietta complaining about the exclusivity for months. People like Susanna and me didn't stand a chance.

"Nick Jansen, the club owner, was in the store today. So I flat out asked him if I could get an invitation to the opening, and he added me to the list right there.

Can you believe it? I told him I had a girlfriend, and he said 'no problem' and wrote plus-one next to my name." She laughed.

"I'm in. I need to let off steam, badly."

"Great. I'll be at your place at seven with food. I can't wait to see your new digs."

Before saying goodbye, I assured her it was just a temporary place until I could find my own apartment. And a job.

Keeping in mind that we were going to the hottest new club in town, I chose my outfit with care. Most of the clothes I'd borrowed were business or practical, but I'd found some sexy ones I liked. Tonight seemed like a good time to break out those.

After some consideration, I settled on a deep purple halter top dress that hugged my curves nicely.

The heatwave we were experiencing this week made it a bad idea to leave my hair down, so I kept it simple. A messy bun, mascara, and candy pink lip gloss were good enough for me.

A buzz from downstairs pulled my attention away from my reflection. After confirming it was Susanna, I buzzed her in and waited for her to knock on my door. When I opened it, Susanna let out a low whistle.

"You're looking pretty good yourself," I said with a warm smile. In her favorite burgundy club dress, she definitely did.

She flashed a bottle of Pinot Grigio in one hand and a large bag of Chinese food in the other. "Got any glasses?"

As we settled with wine, Kung Pao chicken, and spring rolls, it felt like nothing had changed the past few weeks. Once we'd finished the food and wine and placed the dishes in the sink, I wondered if Carson was working late like he usually did. Then again, it was Saturday night. Maybe he actually had a social life. Either way, it wasn't any of my business.

"Ready?" Susanna held out her arm.

Putting Carson out of my mind, I took my friend's arm. "Let's go."

THE PLACE WAS PACKED as we entered, but it had a cool vibe with a smooth Tropical House groove coming from the speakers. Thirst had me going straight for the bar, and after downing half a bottle of water, Susanna leaned in to be heard over the music. "I've missed you," she said. "It's so not the same at work after the Devereaux witches fired you. I'm not sure how much longer I can stand it there." She let out a sigh, then smiled. "Sorry, enough job talk. Come, let's dance."

I took her hand and let her pull me to my feet. "I'm all yours."

She spun me onto the dance floor and put her hands on my hips as we swayed to the beat. As always, we moved well together, our bodies seeming to know where the other was going without a word. A step to the side. A bump of hips.

A DRESS FOR CURVES

At some point, the music shifted to a faster beat. Susanna and I were joined by others, bodies brushing together, smiles given and received. The world was all pulsing sound and moving limbs. A man's hand settled on the small of my back, and he came around my side, giving me a glimpse of rich brown skin and a wide smile.

Then, over his shoulder, someone else caught my eye.

Even in the flashing club lights, I recognized that profile. I never expected to see him here, but there was no mistaking that man. Carson McCrae was sitting at the bar, looking hotter than ever.

As I watched, his head turned, and despite the crowd of people between us, our eyes met. It felt like everything, and everyone around us had disappeared for a moment. Then, I remembered he said our kiss was a mistake.

I gave him a small smile with a nod and turned away. Susanna was dancing with a tall guy now, their bodies plastered together. She raised an eyebrow, and I grinned back.

Suddenly, I found myself across from the handsome man from earlier, and we danced in sync.

He moved in a way that told me he'd be good in bed, but a familiar scent filled my nostrils just as the song ended. A delicious mix of sandalwood, leather, and other masculine aromas had things low inside me, tightening.

"May I cut in?"

I opened my eyes to find Carson. His eyes were dark and unreadable as they moved from me to the guy.

My dance partner gave me a questioning look as I thanked him for the dance, but I didn't second guess my decision.

"Are you sure?" he said. "You don't know what you'll be missing, honey."

"She said, thank you for the dance. Be a good boy and make yourself scarce." Carson's voice was rough, almost a growl.

The guy studied Carson's face for a moment before turning. "She's all yours, old man."

As he walked away, Carson stepped into the space, and his presence filled it all. Then, his hands were on my waist, and all thoughts disappeared. Carson pulled me closer until our bodies nearly touched, and I wrapped my arms around his neck, the gesture as natural as it was desired.

"I didn't interrupt anything, did I?" he asked.

"Not at all," I said. "Just out dancing with a friend." I pointed to Susanna, still with the tall guy. "My old roommate."

"Good. Just wanted to be sure I'm not stepping on anyone's toes," he said.

And then he was kissing me.

Again.

FIFTEEN
CARSON

She tasted like strawberries and rum, sweet and intoxicating. Making a pleased sound, Vix leaned into me, her breasts pressing against my chest. With our bodies flush against each other, I couldn't hide how she affected me, and I didn't want to. I called last night a mistake, but it didn't have to be, not if we were smart about things.

Smart right now meant grinding against her as the music set a pulsing beat designed to inspire sex. One of my hands slid down to her ass and squeezed. She rewarded me with a bite to my bottom lip before soothing the sting with a soft lick.

Fuck.

If my violet-eyed goddess kept that up, I'd come in my pants like some damn teenager.

I gripped her hair and gave a tug, then whispered her name against her lips. Her eyes flicked up to mine, gaze still slightly dazed.

"I want you," I said bluntly. "No strings, no promises, no repercussions or offense taken whatever you decide."

She blinked slowly at me, and I waited for her to process. No matter how badly I wanted her, I wouldn't rush her. We both needed to go into this with our eyes open and expectations properly set. That was the only way this would work without completely screwing up our business relationship.

"Why are you here?" she asked carefully. "Did you know I was coming?"

I shook my head. "I'm friends with the owner. He asked me to come for his opening night. I was just going to stay for one quick drink, then I saw you."

I leaned in for another kiss, quick but thorough enough to leave both of us to be a little breathless. "Come home with me."

"Are you sure that's a good idea?" she asked.

"The best idea I've ever had." I stepped out of her embrace and held out my hand, the invitation clear. She took it without a trace of hesitation, and I led her out of the club.

It took all my self-control to keep my hands to myself on the ride to my apartment. If I hadn't been behind the wheel, I might have done something wild. Like, see how many times I could bring her to orgasm with my fingers.

I worried that the time it took for us to get to my place would dampen the fire between us, make us have second thoughts. Instead, seeing Vix smiling and singing in a charmingly off-key voice made me even more determined to have her.

After pulling into my usual parking space, I went around the car and opened the passenger door for her, holding out a hand. The moment her hand slid into mine, a jolt of electricity went through me. Her head snapped up, her eyes wide. Good. I wasn't the only one who felt it.

Urgency sparked once more as we hurried inside. A new neighbor passed as we entered the lobby, his eyes lighting up when he saw Vix. I glared at him, releasing her hand to wrap my arm around her waist and pull her closer to me. He chuckled and gave me a nod that told me he acknowledged she was mine.

Well, not *mine*, exactly. We didn't have that kind of relationship. We were friends who worked together and were about to have hot, explosive sex.

"Are you having second thoughts?" Vix's voice cut through my musings as we stepped onto the elevator. "I don't want you to be uncomf–"

My lips slammed down on hers, and we stumbled back against the wall. One hand on her ass, the other slid up to cup a breast. She moaned, her hand on my chest, gripping my shirt. I dropped my hand lower, seeking bare skin, and she gasped when I found it. Slipping my fingers under the hem of her skirt, I caressed the back of her thigh, earning another moan.

Then the elevator doors dinged, and I pulled back. Vix's pale skin was flushed as she straightened her clothes, and her kiss-swollen lips were curved into a pleased smile. I took her hand again, raising it to brush a kiss across her knuckles as I led her off the elevator. While I didn't have a whole floor penthouse, my place wasn't small, especially for New York City.

Once inside, I flicked on the light and kicked off my shoes. Out of the corner of my eye, I saw Vix's heels as they came off, and I reached for her.

Keeping eye contact with her, I sank to my knees. Starting at her ankles, I ran my hands up her long, shapely legs, enjoying the little gasps of anticipation that came as I pushed up the bottom of her dress. When I saw the black lace thong she wore, I cursed.

"Did you wear these to show someone tonight?" I asked. I pressed my lips against the inside of her thigh, moving her legs further apart. "Hmm? Did you have anyone specific in mind when you picked them out?"

She shook her head. "I just dressed for me."

I kissed the damp fabric over her mound. "Well, you're gorgeous."

Before she could respond, I pulled aside the crotch of her panties and pressed my mouth against her bare skin. She moaned, and I worked my tongue into her slit, licking down and back up again, paying extra attention to the little bundle of nerves at the top. With a smile, I pulled her leg over my shoulder, opening her more fully. Delicate pink skin glistened, and I gave in to the desire to lick every inch.

As I flicked my tongue back and forth across her clit, she buried her fingers in my hair. Sharp tugs encouraged me to thrust my tongue inside her, to suck on her clit, to kiss her pussy as passionately as her mouth. My grip on her legs tightened, holding her in place as I brought her to climax.

She called out my name, and I smiled at the surge of pride that went through me. I held her until the quivering in her muscles stopped, and then, wiping the back of my hand across my mouth, I stood. That was the first of what would be many orgasms tonight.

I was just getting started.

SIXTEEN
VIX

I would've called Carson out on his smug smile, but my entire body was still tingling from the aftereffects of his hard work, so he earned it. If he hadn't wrapped his arm around my waist when he stood, I would've crumpled right to the floor. He chuckled as he led me through the apartment to a hallway and into his bedroom.

I had a few moments to see a fairly simple-looking space done in neutral shades of brown and green, but it was the king-sized bed that captured my attention for obvious reasons. Then I was tumbling back into it, my grip on Carson's shirt taking him with me.

In a tangle of limbs, we somehow got out of our clothes while stealing kisses that heated me from the inside out. Then his hands were on my bare skin, and my outside was just as hot as my inside.

As distracting as his touch was, the sight of him captivated me. I had an exquisite view of everything

Carson McCrae had been hiding under those perfectly tailored clothes and *damn*.

That fine, long, lean body. His torso was cut, defined, from his pecs to the first legitimate six-pack I'd ever seen. And then there were those deep grooves at his hips that I wanted to lick. A light dusting of hair ran from his chest down in a trail to his belly button and lower. Lower to slightly darker curls that surrounded a long, thick cock curving up toward his stomach. Flushed with blood, it was a couple of shades darker than the rest of his skin, and I had to touch it.

Silk over hot steel, if that made any sense.

Carson cursed, his grip tightening on my hips as every muscle in his body tensed. I ran my fingertips up the full length of his thick shaft, enjoying the way it twitched, the way his body jerked. I looked up to meet his eyes, his pupils blown wide until only a thin ring of pale blue was visible. His heated gaze sent a shiver down my spine.

"Beautiful." I pushed myself up to brush my lips across his as I wrapped my hand around his cock. At the base, my fingers could barely touch, and I couldn't wait to feel it stretching me.

"Vix..." My name was a drawn-out groan.

I kissed his jaw, his throat, all the while teasing and stroking his cock. It thickened under my hand, and my pussy throbbed in anticipation. As good as his mouth was, I knew this would be better. But I wasn't done exploring yet.

I pushed against his chest, getting him to lean back

on his knees as I bent to take him into my mouth, my hands resting on his firm thighs for balance. He caught his breath a split second before my lips closed around his tip. Sucking lightly, I lowered my head, reveling in the primal sounds he made.

Inch by inch, I took him into my mouth, lips stretching wide around him. The heavy weight of him slid over my tongue, his flavor heady. As his cock went deeper, I relaxed my throat until I had all of him.

"Fuck, Vix." His hand landed on my head, fingers digging into my scalp.

I swallowed twice, enjoying the curses spilling from his lips, and then slowly raised my head. Each pull of my mouth, every pass of my tongue, brought out a new noise that sent another rush of arousal through me.

"Stop." He pulled me back, his eyes wide and wild. "I want to be inside you when I come."

"Condom?" My voice was rough, my lips tender.

"Right." He nodded, reaching over to the bedside table.

I leaned back on my elbows and enjoyed the show as Carson slowly rolled the latex over that thick, impressive cock. He truly was a work of art, and I didn't want to share all that yummy goodness with anyone else.

Catching my chin, he crushed his mouth against mine. His tongue stroked mine, plundered my mouth, explored. His free hand covered my breast, squeezing it even as my hardened nipple rubbed against my palm.

Gripping his shoulders, I pulled him down on me, his weight more than welcome between my thighs. The tip of him brushed against my entrance, and I arched against him, eager for him to fill me. I hooked my leg around his hip as I tilted my head and deepened the kiss.

Taking the hint—or just feeling the same desperation as me—he reached between us and, a moment later, buried himself inside me with a single thrust. I cried out, my body freezing for several heartbeats, unable to do anything but feel every overwhelming sensation my nerves were frantically trying to transmit. My heart racing. Blood pumping. My chest tight, and spots dancing in front of my eyes.

"I've got you," Carson murmured the words against my lips, his voice drawing me back. "Breathe, sweetheart. Just breathe."

Oh. Right. Air.

I sucked in a breath, and he chuckled, the vibration making me whimper. Then he moved only an inch back before sliding forward again. All the laughter left his face, and something shifted in the air between us. His eyes locked with mine, and I found myself unable to look away as he pushed into me with smooth, even strokes. Each one went deep, reaching places inside me I didn't think had ever been touched before. With a deliberateness that fit with everything about this man's character, he drove us toward oblivion, every thrust sending a new wave of pleasure washing over me.

As the pace increased, he put his hand on my

cheek, his thumb brushing across the corner of my mouth. Without breaking eye contact, I turned my head just enough to close my lips around his thumb. Carson sucked in a breath, and his rhythm stuttered when I sunk my teeth into the flesh. His break in concentration didn't last long, and then he was pounding into me, taking me to the brink of where pleasure became pain until I tipped over the edge, my vision going gray.

As I slipped into the black, I heard him call my name.

I WAS HOT, and I did not know why. I didn't keep the apartment this warm, and I was pretty sure I was naked. And while I could feel some fabric against my skin, there was also something that didn't feel like a sheet. It was too heavy. Too warm. And...skin.

Shit.

It was skin.

And something hard was pressing against my ass.

My eyes flew open as the night's memories came flooding back.

Fuck.

It was morning, with enough sunlight coming between the curtains to let me see, which meant I fell asleep. I remembered nothing after coming, but now I was curled up against Carson, my back to his front, one arm around my waist, one leg over mine.

I needed to leave.

Now.

My mind raced as I tried to get out from under Carson without waking him. I couldn't complicate this. Not while I was working for him, living in his apartment, and counting on a good reference. And I needed him to know nothing had changed from our original agreement. That this had to be just a onetime thing.

As I got out of the bed, Carson's voice came from behind me. "Morning."

Forcing my body to stay relaxed, I said, "Good morning." I found my bra and dress and pulled them on. I continued, the words coming out in a rush, "Last night was fun, and I like you, but it wouldn't be a good idea to do this again while I'm modeling for you."

"You're right. We can't do this again."

A small part of me—one that I didn't even know existed until that moment—died at his words. I wasn't angry at him for agreeing with me, but I was surprised at the disappointment I felt. A part of me wished he had suggested some way to be together, despite the complications.

But that wouldn't be smart, especially since I did not know if what we had could even become something. I couldn't give up a reliable, certain future for something that might not work out.

Finally finding my panties, I pulled them on, ducking my head to avoid eye contact. "I'll show myself out."

Before he could offer to be chivalrous and get me a car, I hurried toward the door.

This was why everything was better casual. It made life simple. Like it was back home. Well, like it was before *he* arrived. Pyxis Machoi. The person who made me leave my home with no intention of ever returning.

I wasn't leaving this time, though. No matter how awkward things would get, I was in New York City to stay.

SEVENTEEN
CARSON

Something hit my nose and bounced into my glass of lemonade, startling me. My eyes narrowed as I zeroed in on my laughing sister, London.

"What was that for?" I asked, fishing a ball of rolled-up paper out of my drink.

"Saying your name a million times wasn't working," she said, brandy-colored eyes glinting with mischief. "I figured a direct assault would be a better way to get your attention."

"In her defense, she tried talking to you first." Louis spoke up from where he sat next to the infamous Rory, his new boyfriend. The fact that Louis had brought him to dinner with London and me spoke volumes about his feelings for the handsome actor.

"I'm sorry, London," I apologized. "What were you saying?"

London raised an eyebrow. "I was thanking you for convincing me to stick with this role instead of taking that understudy offer. I heard that the Pretty Woman tour is getting poor reviews."

"I just helped you see what you already knew," I said. I looked over at Rory. "My sister is an exceptionally talented actor. You should see her perform sometime."

"Carson," London hissed as she kicked me under the table. Color flooded her cheeks. "I'm so sorry, Mr. Kent. My brother can be an idiot sometimes."

"It's okay." Rory laughed. "I have an older sister who's extremely proud of her theater geek brother. And it's Rory, please."

London beamed. "Thanks, Rory." She glanced at me and then at Louis. "Can I just say that you were brilliant in the Miss Saigon revival and totally should have won."

"Thank you." Rory gave her a warm smile. "Is it too cliché to say that it was an honor just to be nominated?"

"I'd be thrilled to be nominated for a Tony one day." She closed her eyes and smacked herself in the forehead. "That sounded really petty and envious, didn't it?"

"Not at all," Rory said. "It sounded like someone who appreciates being recognized for her craft." He looked at me. "I'm sure you can understand, Carson. We might not have the same medium, but we're all artists."

"The first time Carson got a mention in Vogue, he made me go buy fifty copies," Louis said.

"I did not." I pointed at him. "I asked you to buy a few so I could send them to my family."

"You framed the article."

I laughed and nodded. "You're right. I did do that."

"Now, London, I have a question for you," Rory said. "Why did you turn down the Pretty Woman role? Are you against doing a tour?"

"No, I actually would love to, if it's a good role," she said. "And I'm not a diva. It doesn't have to be the lead or anything. Just a good part."

"What are your thoughts on Les Misérables?"

London's eyes went wide. "It's one of my favorite shows. Eponine is my dream role."

Rory leaned forward. "I just talked to a friend earlier today who said they're casting for a new national tour within the next couple of weeks. From what he said, they're doing an open casting call."

"Really?" The excitement in my sister's voice made me smile.

"I'll be auditioning myself," Rory continued. "If you'd like, we can rehearse lines together."

"I would love that," London said.

"If you've never done a tour before," he said, "you should know it's different from doing a show here. I can give you some pointers."

As the two of them continued talking about the ins and outs of casting calls on Broadway, I leaned back and enjoyed not having to think for once. I appreciated being able to turn my brain off and just listen.

When, a quarter of an hour later, after London

excused herself to the restroom and Rory stepped out for a cigarette, I raised my hand for the check.

"I like him," I said to Louis. "He's a good guy."

"He is to die for." Louis got a dreamy look on his face. "You know, I think I'm going to tell him I want us to be exclusive."

My eyebrows shot up. "Exclusive? Seriously?"

"It's time to settle down with a steady boyfriend."

I almost choked on my wine. In the entire time I'd known Louis, he'd never been exclusive with anyone.

"I never thought you'd limit yourself to one guy," I admitted. "You always seemed like you loved playing the field."

"True," Louis said. "This is all new to me, but when I'm with Rory, I don't want to be with anyone else. Hell, I haven't even looked at another man in over a month." He shook his head. "I know it's crazy, but I just want him."

I was shocked. I'd never imagined Louis giving up his freedom to do whatever he wanted, with whoever he wanted. I guess I always thought of Louis as being single forever.

Just like me.

EIGHTEEN
VIX

Coming in on Monday, I braced for the worst.

It was always weird seeing someone again after having been naked together, but it was a hundred times worse, considering I also worked for him.

"Good, you're here. Just in time for the video call," Carson said, his expression and tone perfectly polite.

We moved to his desktop, where he turned on his computer. Two people appeared on the screen.

"Hi guys," Carson said. "How are you today?"

"Chuffed to hear how things are going," Baylen said.

"Vix, this is Baylen McFann and Harlee Sumpter. Guys, this is Vixen Teal, the face and body of our campaign."

"I remember you," Baylen said with a smile. "Harlee and I met you when we were in the city."

"That's right," I said. "It was a boiling day."

I sounded like an idiot talking about the weather.

"Vix won't be our only model, of course," Carson announced, "but she'll close out the show with the bra and the matching underwear. Then, we'll reveal that all the models have been wearing the new bra under their outfits. Since we're using models of all different shapes and sizes, it'll show the versatility."

As the conversation turned to the various designs, I watched Carson talking to Baylen and Harlee more than I listened to what they were saying. Every time I looked at him, all I could think about was how it felt to have him touch me, kiss me, and how I couldn't stop myself from wanting more.

Shit.

When the call ended, he turned to me, and I wanted to be anywhere else but here. Anywhere that didn't have the object of my fascination within reaching distance.

"That went well. I think they liked you." He smiled and stepped into the kitchenette for another coffee. "I almost forgot. I talked to a couple of friends of mine yesterday about the exclusive boutique they're opening. They haven't advertised for any positions yet, but I'll recommend you if you're interested in working there."

"Really?" I shouldn't have been so surprised. He'd been nothing but kind to me, and he had already offered to be my reference on applications.

"Of course." He almost looked offended, and I felt a stab of guilt.

A DRESS FOR CURVES

"Thank you," I blurted out. "I'd appreciate it very much."

He gave me a nod and then went to a nearby table. After jotting down some information, he held out a piece of paper.

"Here's the number to call. Tell them I gave it to you."

Thanking him again, I put the paper in my pocket and almost wished I had a valid excuse to stick around. But that would be tempting fate. Being this close to the show, the best thing was to not be around him at all. Who says we couldn't pick it up from where we'd left off? Once I no longer modeled for him, a business relationship wouldn't be an issue.

Who was I kidding? Why would a gorgeous and extremely successful man like Carson McCrae want to be with someone like me? He had an initial attraction to me that led to sex, but that's all. If there was one thing I knew about attractions, they always faded...fast.

NINETEEN
CARSON

I cursed under my breath and shifted to get a better angle to place a pin. The dress had given me problems, and with the show approaching soon, I could feel the pressure. Fortunately, it only needed a few minor tweaks, most of which were cosmetic touches.

"Carson?"

Vix's voice made my heart leap, and I struggled to keep my voice even. "In here." The pins in my mouth dropped to the floor, and I cursed again.

"Are you all right?" The question held the concern I could see on Vix's expression as she came into the studio.

"I'm fine." I smiled at what I hoped was polite reassurance. "Just working on a dress for the show."

"And you're doing that from the floor?" She raised an eyebrow. "Couldn't you just put the mannequin up higher so you could sit in a chair or stand?"

"I could," I agreed, "but where would the fun be in that?"

She laughed and held out a hand. I took it, trying to ignore the thrill that went through me from that bit of physical contact.

"I brought you dinner." She held up a bag I hadn't noticed. "I thought you'd probably be working late."

As if prompted by her words, my stomach growled loudly. We both laughed, and the last of the tension between us disappeared.

"Join me?" I gestured toward the kitchenette area of the studio. "Unless you've already eaten?"

"I haven't," she said as I placed the bags on the counter.

She went to the fridge. "Drink?"

"I'll take a beer."

I opened the bag to see three containers of Vietnamese food. My favorite. "Fork or chopsticks?"

"Chopsticks," she said. "My mother went through a stage where rice was all we ate for a year, so I learned to wield the two wooden sticks."

"Was that a normal thing growing up?" I asked. "Your mom going on food kicks like that?"

"All the time." Vix brought over two bottles of beer, handing me one before taking a seat next to me. "I didn't exactly have a traditional childhood."

"I've told you about my crazy family tree, right?" I gently teased.

"You have." She gave me a partial smile. "But I think mine can beat yours."

"Oh really?" I tipped the neck of my beer toward her in a challenge. "Go for it."

"I grew up in a commune a few hours from here," she said. "Very non-traditional. We were not divided into families. Like, I didn't grow up with my biological parents. The entire village was my family, and some kids didn't even know who both of their parents were."

A commune. Huh. Not what I expected. Then, a thought occurred to me, and I frowned. "Wait, so you grew up in a commune where not everybody knew their relations. What happened if you thought some guy was cute? How would you know if you were related to him?"

She laughed, her cheeks pink. "Of course, we knew. We were careful if we were the least uncertain."

The idea of a teenage Vix flirting with horny teenage boys twisted my stomach. I almost wanted to ask how many guys I needed to be jealous of. Instead, I turned the conversation back to family.

"Any biological siblings?"

She nodded. "Two brothers and a sister on my mom's side, and a sister and a brother, Wulf, on my father's side. Wulf still lives there. He's about your age. My sister from my mom, Antoinette, is there too."

"Are you guys close?" I asked before taking another tasty mouthful of Banh xeo.

"Sort of. More Wulf than Antoinette. He and I got close after his daughter, Andrea, was born. She's adorable. I loved her from the first time I held her."

I smiled, remembering holding my niece Evanne at the hospital. "When was the last time you saw her?"

Vix's smile faded, and she didn't answer. Instead, she asked about my family.

I didn't want to push her to answer my question, so we talked about me. For a moment, I found it on the tip of my tongue to ask her if she wanted to accompany me to a charity event coming up. Some of my family would be there, and I could introduce her.

Fortunately, I caught myself in time. Vix wasn't my girlfriend. As long as she worked for me, this was as far as things could go. No matter how much I wanted to be with her again. And again.

TWENTY

VIX

"Carson told us you worked two years at *Soie et Velours*." Yasmin Singh, the elegant businesswoman behind the desk, glanced at my resume. "But he didn't say why you're no longer there."

I clenched my hands together but tried not to let any tension bleed into my voice. I just hoped they would believe my side of things as I told the story of what happened after Karen Devereaux ordered me to bring an envelope to Carson McCrae.

Dasia Smythe, the other co-owner of the boutique, pursed her lips. "I've known Karen since elementary school."

My stomach dropped at her words.

Shit.

"She was as...*unpleasant* then as she is now." Dasia's ice-blue eyes thawed as she looked at me. "I bet Karen has been making it difficult for you to get hired anywhere else."

Relief flooded me, my shoulders slumping. "Yes. Definitely. The two of them verbally assaulted me the other day as I filled out a job application at a boutique."

Yasmin made a disgusted sound. "That woman is a menace. She and her bloody daughter." She looked at Dasia. "And don't tell me I need to be professional. We both know the Devereaux women don't deserve professional courtesy."

Dasia held up a hand. "I wouldn't dream of it."

Yasmin turned back to me, coal-black eyes dancing with humor. "As you can see, we don't give Karen Devereaux's opinion much weight. Any weight, actually."

"We know you're modeling for Carson in his upcoming show, but we can work your schedule around that," Dasia said. "Since you've worked retail before, most of your training will be to familiarize you with our software and our products."

Hope flared, and I struggled to keep it tamped down until I understood her correctly. "Does that mean—I mean, it sounds like–"

"We'd like you to come work for us," Yasmin said. "If that's what you want."

"Yes!" I clapped both my hands over my mouth as I practically yelled the word. Both Dasia and Yasmin laughed, but there wasn't any meanness to it.

This was really happening.

And it was all thanks to Carson McCrae.

A DRESS FOR CURVES

I PRACTICALLY DANCED out of the boutique.

Modeling for Carson was a sort of fairy tale. Wonderful, but not completely real. I needed stability to survive on my own. A regular job I could count on, with a paycheck every month.

I wanted to celebrate my new job, and I knew someone who was always game for dinner and a drink, even in the middle of the week.

She answered on the second ring.

"Susanna? Hey, you're not working tonight, are you?"

"No, I'm off at four. Why?"

"How about I take you out to dinner, and then maybe we go to a club for a bit?"

"What happened?"

I couldn't hold back my excitement. "I just got hired at a new boutique.

Susanna let out a squeal that made me laugh. "Yes! Let's celebrate tonight. That's exactly what I need after the week I've had so far. Where are we going?"

"I'm not sure yet," I said. "But I'll pick you up at the apartment at five."

We said our goodbyes, and as I hung up, I realized that I'd been walking. I found myself at the entrance to the subway. My stomach clenched and my heart pounded as I looked at the stairs in front of me.

I slowly backed away, focusing on taking deep breaths. As I calmed, I realized I couldn't do it. I just couldn't take the subway. Even the thought of it had me stressed.

I hated being scared and hated that what happened would keep me from living my life without fear, but I couldn't bring myself down those stairs. Maybe one day, but not today.

I walked to the curb to hail a cab.

I would go back to the apartment, change my clothes into something gorgeous, and then go out with my friend and celebrate all the good things that had happened to me since the dreadful day my life changed.

TWENTY-ONE
CARSON

THERE'S A SAYING THAT GOES SOMETHING LIKE this, if you do what you love, you'll never work a day in your life. That was a lie. Sometimes work was work, no matter how much a person liked it. And occasionally, it was the most frustrating thing in the world.

Today was one of those days.

I was woken when the bloody fire alarm went off.

That meant an evacuation without the elevators. One of the few times living near the top of the building sucked.

It was a false alarm, but we still had to stand outside in the rain while the fire department checked every floor.

Forty minutes later, I joined a handful of other sodden tenants in the now-working elevators. Tenants and two equally wet and bad-tempered yapping dogs.

One of them pissed on my leg.

After a shower–during which I ran out of soap–

and a shave–which resulted in three nasty nicks–I drove to work. Since I was late, I took a shortcut and lost another hour because of an accident that blocked all traffic.

It's fair to say that I wasn't in the best mood when I got to the studio.

As I sat down at my desk, I reached for my phone to see a note reminding me that Vix would be here shortly for her last fitting before the show on Saturday.

I completely forgot she was coming in today. I was glad Dasia and Yasmin hired her, but I couldn't deny I missed seeing her around.

Finally, my day was looking up.

I fetched the dresses for her as I waited with excitement. Except afternoon turned to evening, and she still wasn't here.

"I'm so sorry I'm late," Vix apologized as she rushed into the room, her cheeks flushed. "We were putting some last-minute touches on a window display when a pigeon, of all things, got into the–"

"I don't need excuses," I snapped. "I just need you to honor the commitment you made for *this* job like you promised."

Vix froze. Everything about her going still. The shock on her face made my stomach twist.

Shit.

Her reaction didn't last long. She gave herself a visible shake. "What do you want me to wear first?"

I pointed, not trusting myself to talk. Vix didn't

look at me as she took the dress and disappeared into the back.

I raked a hand through my hair and turned from the direction she'd gone.

Pull yourself together, man.

Maybe it was better that she wasn't around as much anymore. Better that she worked at the boutique.

If I didn't see her, I couldn't fuck up things. Never mind trying to explain how I felt.

How *could* I explain? I didn't understand it myself.

TWENTY-TWO
VIX

IF SOMEONE HAD ASKED ME A MONTH AGO WHICH was harder, working retail or modeling, I probably would've said retail. Today, however, I put modeling way higher on the difficulty scale. Standing still while being primped and prodded was a lot more challenging than it looked. Stepping out onto a catwalk with all eyes on you and everyone searching for the tiniest flaw was nerve-wracking. Trying not to trip and make a fool of yourself was another daunting task. Struggling not to get lost in the thousands of possibilities of where things would go next with a certain gorgeous designer...

Okay, that last one was just me. I hoped, anyway.

Carson was busy and focused as he hurried around backstage, making last-second adjustments. He didn't make eye contact or speak to anyone outside of brisk instructions, but I assumed that was usual, judging by the lack of concern my fellow models showed.

I felt anything but normal. I would be the center of

attention in a few minutes, which wasn't something I'd ever imagined. I wasn't shy, but there was a big difference between being social and enjoying the spotlight. I was the former, not the latter, and was now wondering what had possessed me to agree to this.

"You're up." Derry, one of Carson's other models, wasn't working today, but she had come in to support the rest of us, and I was grateful for her friendly face as she gave me a gentle nudge toward the stage.

The next couple of hours passed with the same blur that accompanied my busy day yesterday at the boutique opening.

Finally, I was down to my last outfit—if it could be called that—and Carson was announcing the unveiling of his new bra.

The bra and matching panty set were made in a rich, royal purple and silk rather than the lace option, and they were definitely sexy. Although Carson had seen me in them before, I still glanced his way to see if he thought I looked good. Not model good, but sexy good. I wanted to see the admiration in his eyes, even if only a bit of surface lust.

The utterly blank look on his face hit me harder than I liked, and I realized I'd been naive to think that maybe when I no longer was modeling for Carson, he would want to date me.

How stupid of me.

As soon as I made it backstage, I grabbed the dress Carson had made for me and pulled it on. I wanted to go home and curl up on the couch with a good book, but I couldn't. My job wasn't done yet. There was an after-party, and we were all expected to attend.

However, I could still try to avoid Carson for the rest of the evening. I would make my escape as soon as politely acceptable and then stay as far away from the studio as possible. With any luck, I could find my own place before the end of the month, and that would be that.

I was still telling myself that nearly two hours later when my cheeks ached from smiling so hard. Only Derry kept me sane, checking in with me twice as often as the other models.

Still, there came the point when I needed a break, and I seized an opportunity to duck into a little alcove where a giant potted plant shielded me from view.

Just then, a painfully familiar brittle laugh came from a few feet away. I bristled at the sound.

Brietta Devereaux.

It surprised me that Carson had invited the Devereauxes, but then again, it was his show. He could ask anyone he wanted.

I ignored her and tried to pass, but she stepped right in my path.

"You know what's funny, Vix?" Brietta said with a smirk. "For the longest time, I couldn't figure out why Carson would hire *you* as one of his models. Out of all the women in Manhattan, he picked you. Now I know. He wanted to show the world he's capable of designing clothing that flatters even ugly, fat women like you.

The man is a genius." She shook her head. "Such a shame that he swings the other way, though."

My hands clenched into fists. I didn't mind Brietta insulting me, but the other women deserved better. And what did she mean by 'swings the other way'?

"You think it's true, then?" The young man next to Brietta appeared to be hanging on her every word. "That he's gay?"

"It has to be," she said. "It's the only logical explanation. I flirted with him once, and he turned me down flat. Only a total fag would do that."

My jaw dropped. It wasn't the fact that Brietta assumed only a gay man would turn her down that had my blood boiling. It was *that* word she used.

"You mean no straight guy's ever turned you down?" the young man asked.

"Would you?" Brietta practically purred.

"Hell, no!"

I closed my eyes and let out a slow breath. Confronting Brietta here wouldn't be a good idea.

"Luckily, I've never agreed to work with him," Brietta continued. "It creeps me out thinking about him touching me."

"I don't understand," the guy said. "Why would that be creepy if he's not trying to hit on you?"

"It's disgusting, that's why." Brietta sneered. "You would agree, unless you're a fucking faggot, too."

"Me?!" His voice cracked. "Hell, no!"

I didn't wait to hear anything else he might say. Or

if Brietta would add to the insults she was spewing. I'd heard enough.

"You should be ashamed of yourself." I kept my voice even despite the emotions roiling inside me. "Not just for running your mouth about things you don't understand, but for using words that no decent human being would ever let come out of their mouth."

Brietta looked shocked, but that didn't last long. Fury came next, and a lot of it.

"How dare you?!" Her voice rose above the surrounding conversation. "You can't talk to me like that! You were nothing when my mom hired you! Less than nothing!"

I looked at her, wondering how big a scene she would make this time. She glanced at the young man gaping at the two of us and answered my unasked question by throwing her glass of wine in my face.

"Fat bitch!"

TWENTY-THREE

CARSON

What the hell?!

I was doing the usual meet and greet when it happened. To ensure all the clients, vendors, and other customers had my full attention at the afterparty, I'd avoided Vix all night, but I'd kept her on my radar.

Suddenly, I heard Brietta yelling and turned just in time to see her throw a glass of wine at Vix.

"Enough!" I stepped between Vix and Brietta, my voice catching the attention of everyone around me. "Brietta, you need to leave. Now."

"Get away from me!" Brietta hissed, her eyes narrowing.

"My daughter did nothing wrong."

Dammit.

Karen Devereaux appeared at Brietta's side and pointed at Vix. "That *horrible woman* insulted my daughter! She should be thrown out immediately!"

I looked at the guy standing next to Brietta, his eyes

wide with shock. I didn't know his name, but I recognized him. He was the son of one of my distributors. Jim Williams. That must have been how the Devereauxes got here. I certainly didn't invite them.

"You saw everything. Tell me what happened."

"Um." His face flooded with color, and his gaze darted around as if searching for an escape.

"Don't you dare." Brietta glared at him.

I noticed a small sliver of white power under his nose. I grabbed a napkin from a tray and handed it to him. "You got a little something under your nose there. That's a nasty habit." I narrowed my eyes thoughtfully. "You know, I saw your father earlier. Maybe he'll know what to do about that little habit of yours. Should I give him your best when I see him again?" I asked, my tone casual.

The guy gulped and shook his head.

That was good because I probably wasn't seeing his dad for months.

"Just tell me the truth," I said. "That's all I want, no matter how ugly it is."

He nodded. "All right." He glanced at Brietta and Karen, who scowled at him. "Brietta was just talking about how you're...you know."

"Let's say I don't know."

"That you, uh, play for the other team." His face turned red. "You know...a f-faggot." His gaze darted to my face before going back down to his hands. "And she said she was glad she never modeled for you because it was disgusting, thinking about you touching her."

I'd heard the rumors that had followed me all my life. They still pissed me off. "Is that so?"

"You can't seriously be considering taking *his* word for it," Karen sputtered.

I ignored her. "What happened next?"

"That woman," he pointed at Vix, "told Brietta she should be ashamed for saying that, and Brietta threw the wine in her face."

"Thank you," I said to him before turning my attention to mother and daughter. "You need to leave."

"Excuse me?" Karen pointed at me. "You have no right–"

"I have every right," I cut in. "Besides the fact that this is my event, and you assaulted one of my models, I invited neither of you to the show n*or* the party."

"We assumed our invitation got lost in the mail." Brietta folded her arms. "After all, no one would *dare* snub us like that."

A tight smile settled on my lips. "*I* dare. Get the fuck out."

I knew that we had an audience, but I no longer cared about anything but getting these women as far away from Vix as possible. I was done playing nice. If that cost me some connections, it was a sacrifice I was willing to make.

Both Karen and Brietta were flushed, and neither looked like they had any intention of leaving.

"Security," I called out.

"You wouldn't," Karen said, fury emanating from every pore.

"I would, and I am," I countered. "One more thing, stay the hell away from Vix."

"That b–"

I didn't let her finish. "Get out."

For a few seconds, I worried the Devereauxes would act out, maybe make a scene terrible enough to call the cops. Then Elwood stepped between them, and both women stared at him, suddenly seeming to realize I was serious.

I watched as Elwood led them out, and only as they disappeared did I finally look around for Vix.

But she was gone.

TWENTY-FOUR
VIX

"Dammit, dammit, dammit!" I watched the red wine stain spreading across the fabric, muttering curses under my breath and fighting back the tears.

I barely remembered getting from the main floor to the bathroom. Seeing Carson as Brietta threw the wine on me was my last clear memory. Somewhere in that daze, I made my way to the bathroom down the hallway. There, I stripped down to my panties and began the process of saving Carson's hard work from being ruined.

"Hey, can I come in?"

Derry's voice came from the other side of the door.

Relief cut through my panic, and I rushed to open the door. Her eyes widened, and I remembered I was practically naked.

"I come bearing gifts," she said as she ducked into the bathroom and shut the door.

"Salt." Derry held up a saltshaker. "I stole it from the buffet table."

I stared at her. "Why? Are we doing tequila shots?"

"Shut up, girl. Best thing to use on a wine stain." Derry grinned at me. "I'm a fountain of knowledge, though tequila would be nice."

"Well, go at it," I said. I gestured toward the clothes. "Please."

Derry got to work sprinkling salt on the stained area. I watched as she made a thin layer over the area, and as I focused on that, the bright edge of panic receded.

"Thank you so much," I said. "I never would've thought of using salt."

"Carson actually taught me." Derry put the salt shaker on the counter. "Now, you wanna tell me what happened?"

I gave her a summary, and when I finished, she squeezed my hand.

"You're a good woman for standing up to that bitch."

I shrugged it off, embarrassed. "Anyone would've done it."

"No, you're too modest," she said.

A knock on the door interrupted before I could respond.

"Vix?"

Carson.

Derry went to the door.

"Derry? I thought Vix was in there."

"She is."

I turned as Derry opened the door wider. The surprise on Carson's face was a clue, and I moved to cover up.

"I see you're in good hands."

He turned to go, but Derry caught his arm and yanked him into the bathroom. "Don't be an idiot," she said mildly. "She needs you more."

Then Derry walked out and closed the door, leaving me alone with Carson.

And I was still mostly naked.

I did, however, regain my composure enough to push aside my self-consciousness. "I'm sorry about that."

"About what?" he asked as he stepped toward me.

"I honestly don't know," I chuckled. "I was afraid the wine Brietta threw would stain, and Derry suggested salt might help."

"It will." Carson's shoulders slumped. After a moment, he motioned to the clothes behind me. "May I?"

"Please." I stepped aside to let him pass, grateful that the space was at least big enough for him to walk by without touching me.

He studied the fabric for a minute and said, "Thank God for Derry," before turning his attention to me. He took a step toward me. "Now, how are you holding up?"

"Fine," I blurted out. "It's not like Brietta hit me."

His expression went dark. "When she threw the wine at you, I couldn't get there fast enough."

"I can't believe she did that," I said, trying not to read anything into what he said. "I mean, she knew I was wearing a dress you designed. All that hard work you put into it."

"Vix." He put his hand on my arm, and heat flooded me. "I wasn't thinking about the dress."

"You weren't?" The question was barely a whisper.

"When I saw what Brietta did...I wanted to protect *you*."

I swallowed hard.

"Brietta and her mom are no longer in the building, and they won't be coming back," he continued. "I told them they were no longer welcome at any of my future events, and I said it loud enough, I wouldn't be surprised if more people in the industry cut ties with them."

"Really?"

"Really." He moved his hand from my arm to my cheek, and I leaned into the touch.

"It will not hurt your business?"

His lips curved up in a sweet smile. "Of course not. Even if it would, it was worth it."

I could hear the sincerity in his voice, see it in his eyes.

"Thank you."

His thumb brushed the side of my mouth. "The show's officially done."

I nodded. "It is."

"You're technically not working for me anymore."

"I'm not."

His eyes locked onto mine. "I want to kiss you."

I didn't need to think of how to respond. "I want you to kiss me."

A light too fierce to be called mere happiness blazed in his eyes as he bent his head. Crushing his lips against mine, he hauled me up against him, my nipples chafing against his jacket, every inch of my skin wholly aware of how little of his was accessible. All my pent-up desire and frustration came pouring out as I leaned into him. When his tongue teased the seam of my mouth, I opened to him, groaning at the taste of champagne and caviar. One hand tangled in my hair, and the other dropped to my ass, squeezing and kneading the muscle there.

My head spun, and my lungs burned, screaming for oxygen. Reluctantly, I pulled back enough to breathe, but I didn't go far, running my lips along his jaw, the slight stubble there rough against my sensitive skin.

"I want you." His voice was almost a growl, the sound downright primal.

And insanely hot.

I nipped at his throat in response and let out a yelp of surprise as his hand came down on my ass with a loud crack. He stilled, and I looked up to see a wary expression as he waited for my response. Keeping my eyes locked with his, I bit his neck again, and he immediately rewarded me with another smack. A shiver went through me.

Suddenly, he spun me around, and I caught myself against the edge of the sink. When he curved his body around mine, he rested his chin on my shoulder, meeting my gaze in our reflection. He cupped my breasts, teasing my nipples into even harder points with talented fingers. When he pushed against me, I could feel how hard he was, how much he wanted me.

"Just say yes, and I'll be inside you," he promised. "I'll make you want to scream my name and enjoy every second you struggle to stay quiet. It won't be slow and sweet. It'll be hard and fast, but I'll get you off. You just have to say yes."

"Yes!" Color flooded my face as I blurted it out.

Then his hands were gone, and I almost protested before I heard the familiar rustle of a condom wrapper.

"Are you wet, sweetheart?" he asked, sliding a hand down the front of my panties. A single finger stroked between my lips, and we both groaned. "Oh, baby, you are. So wet for me."

I nodded, unable to speak. What we shared last time was intense, but this? Sheer desperation and raw need.

He nudged my legs further apart, and I felt him move my panties aside with the hand that wasn't already busy with my throbbing clit. The blunt head of him pushed against my entrance, and I shifted, changing the angle so that he could slide right in.

My eyes closed as my body struggled to process the

fullness that came with having something so large suddenly inside me. Carson moved, withdrawing almost completely before thrusting back inside with a force that drove the air from my lungs. With two fingers making tight circles on my clit and each stroke sending a ripple of pleasure through me, it didn't take long for me to feel that familiar pressure building up.

"Come on, baby." He leaned forward and scraped his teeth along my shoulder blade. "Come for me. Come on my cock."

I shuddered at his words. Something about them twisted me up and turned me on to the point where I tipped over the edge. Biting down on the side of my hand, I gave myself over to the pure ecstasy rolling over and through me. He quickly followed, his arms wrapped around me, face pressed against my back, cock buried deep inside me, and I had the brief but clear thought I wouldn't walk away this time.

I could only hope he felt the same way.

TWENTY-FIVE
CARSON

I'd lost the ability to form words. The last coherent thing I said was Vix's name, and that had been more of a groan when I climaxed. As I fixed myself back in my pants, the reality of what had just happened hit me. I did not know where to go next.

No, that wasn't entirely true. I knew where *I* wanted things to go, but I did not know if Vix was on the same page.

"Wow." Vix broke the silence. "That was...wow."

Her words made it easier for me. "Yeah, it was."

I was a fucking wordsmith.

She chuckled. "Usually, after sex, I would get dressed. But that's not exactly an option unless I want to wear wet clothes."

"Oh, damn, I'm sorry." I shrugged out of my suit jacket. "Here."

She raised one pale eyebrow. "I'm not walking back out there in just your jacket and panties."

Most people here already saw her in a bra and panties an hour ago, but I wasn't about to give the audience more fantasy fodder.

It was surprising. Being proprietary was never really my thing, but with Vix, something had changed.

"I'll get you something to wear," I said.

"And then?"

I brushed the back of my hand down her cheek. "I didn't scare you, did I? Get too rough?"

The surprise in her eyes told me her answer before she said it. "Nope. I enjoyed it."

"I feel like I can let go with you," I admitted. "That doesn't happen to me often. Or, ever, really."

Her cheeks turned pink, a pleased expression on her face. "Then this wasn't a one-time, heat-of-the-moment thing?"

"Only if *you* want it to be," I said. "Or you could spend the night with me. If you want to."

"I'd like that a lot." Her voice was soft.

"Good." I leaned down and brushed my lips across hers. "I'll be right back."

A few minutes later, I returned with another dress and a white version of the bra. After Vix dressed, I feared she might have changed her mind. Instead, she took my hand, threading her fingers between mine.

"Your place or mine?" she asked. "Though, technically, they're both yours."

I chuckled at the teasing note in her voice, warmth pooling in my belly. "Let's go to mine. I have a bigger shower."

A DRESS FOR CURVES

"I THINK I'M IN LOVE." Vix sighed as she stood under the hot spray and rinsed her hair.

I leaned against the heated tile walls, watching. The shared shower was my idea, but not because I had shower sex on the brain. While I was confident we both would've enjoyed it, I had something else in mind, and I wanted to take my time with it.

But that didn't mean I couldn't enjoy the view. Vix's gorgeous body and the sexy sounds she made were having a visible effect on my body. Half-hard, I took my cock in hand, lazily stroking it as I made my plans. I was still doing that when Vix opened her eyes and saw me.

"Like what you're seeing?" She ran her hands over her curves, and my gaze followed, taking in the swell of her breasts with their peach nipples, her soft stomach, rounded hips, the bare, pink skin between her legs.

"Very much." I took a step toward her and held out my hand. "Let me show you."

She took my hand and followed me from the shower. After wrapping her hair in a towel, she let me pat her dry with one of my thickest, fluffiest towels, which turned out to be one of the worst forms of torture. It took all my self-control not to take her right there on the floor.

By the time I finished drying myself off, my libido had calmed down again. I was ready to follow through with my plans.

"I think I have a hairdryer around here somewhere," I said.

"Don't worry about it," Vix said as she tied off her braid. "I don't want to wait that long."

The heat in her eyes dried up anything else I might've said, and I grabbed her hand, practically dragging her into my bedroom. I tugged off the towel she had wrapped around her and gave her a gentle nudge toward the bed. As she situated herself at the head of the bed, I tossed my towel next to hers and then crawled up the bed.

"Spread your legs," I demanded.

She did, stretching her arms out along my pillows, putting her entire gorgeous body on display. I took a minute to admire her, and I was struck again by how beautiful she was.

"If I do anything you don't like, tell me," I said.

"I will." Her mouth curved into a wicked smile that made my blood run hotter. "But I don't think that'll be an issue."

Positioning myself between her legs, I palmed her hips, holding her as I kissed the inside of one thigh, then the other. She sighed, and I kissed higher, taking my time as I moved toward my goal. Gentle kisses against soft flesh made her squirm, and I chuckled before running my tongue along one side and then the other. When I blew lightly on the damp skin, goosebumps broke out all over her.

"I'm going to taste you." I kept my voice low, but I knew she could hear me. "You're going to come on my tongue, sweetheart. And then you're going to come on my fingers. And only after I bring you twice will I finally slide inside that tight pussy of yours and fuck you until you can't remember your name."

"Yes, please." Her breathless words held no hesitation.

I pressed my mouth against her, my tongue licking between her folds, plundering and exploring every inch. The taste of her was as delicious as I remembered.

My tongue found her clit, teased it. Quick flicks back and forth before I pressed the flat of my tongue against that bit of silken flesh. I was a quick study and paid attention to what women liked. And I'd paid specific attention to what Vix wanted.

"Carson," Vix whimpered as her hands came down on my head. "Please, baby, I need to come."

Baby? I smirked. I couldn't think of the last time a woman called me that. Locking my lips around her clit, I switched from friction to suction and was rewarded with a long, drawn-out keen.

Vix's back arched, her fingers digging into my hair. Her muscles quivered under my hands. She was close. As I coaxed her higher, it took all my self-control not to rub my aching cock against the bedspread underneath me. The scent of her surrounded me, twisting up my insides in a mass of want and need, not just for my pleasure, but for hers. I needed her to come. Not because I wanted release, but because she was mine to care for.

For now, anyway.

A few seconds later, I was rewarded with a cry of pleasure as Vix reached her climax. Her thighs clamped down on the sides of my head, her entire body going stiff. Her grip on my hair tightened, and then her legs fell open, her hands dropping to her sides.

I pushed two fingers inside her, and she shouted my name. Swiping the back of my free hand across my mouth, I shifted my position to watch her face as I drove my fingers into her with a slight twisting motion that let my knuckles brush against her g-spot. And with every thrust, my thumb pushed against her clit.

"Carson," she whimpered, her hands scrabbling against the bedspread. "I don't—I don't—I can't–"

"Yes, you can," I countered. "You're going to come on my fingers."

"I need I need I need–"

"I know what you need, sweetheart." I slid my index finger into my mouth, wetting it liberally before dropping it down below my other hand.

She gasped the moment the tip of my finger pressed against her anus, but she didn't pull away or tell me to stop. I kept my eyes on her as I exerted the smallest bit of pressure, continuing to move my other two fingers in and out of her pussy. When my finger sank past that tight ring of muscle to my first knuckle, Vix tensed, and I paused that hand's movement, letting her get used to what appeared to be a new sensation.

"Someday, I'm going to fuck this tight little ass," I promised. "Not now, but soon. And you're going to come stretched out around my cock, begging me to fuck you harder."

The shudder that went through her told me she liked that idea, and that was enough for me to put aside that I just made promises for the future. I wanted more than tonight, but this wasn't the time for a discussion. She relaxed again, which was my cue to continue.

Curling my fingers, I found that spot inside her and lightly rubbed it. As she moaned, I twisted my other finger, moving it deeper inside her ass. It took some concentration to keep my hands moving in different ways, but the sounds coming from Vix were more than worth it. She writhed, hips jerking, almost as if she wanted to get away, but her words said that wasn't the case.

"Let go, baby." I encouraged her. "I know you want to come."

She bit her bottom lip as her head tilted back, giving me a breath-taking view of flushed and perfect breasts. I fully intended to taste those again as soon as I brought her with my fingers. My gut clenched.

"C'mon, Vix." My voice was rougher than usual. "I want to get my cock into this tight cunt of yours, but you have to come first."

I didn't know if it was my words that tipped her over the edge or the right amount of pressure, but she came suddenly.

Her body was still trembling when I came back from the bathroom, condom already on. She didn't look done yet, if the heat in her eyes was any sign. She held out a hand.

Taking it, I settled into the cradle of her thighs and slid home.

Then Vix pulled my head down for a kiss. My needs took precedence, and based on how Vix raised her hips to meet every thrust, she needed it, too. I didn't think it was solely that she wanted another orgasm. It was this connection we had, this feeling of fitting together as if made for each other.

Every touch set me on fire. Every stroke sent a shock of pleasure across my nerves. It radiated up my spine, filled every cell of my body. And when I finally exploded, the world turned into pure, white light.

And she was right there with me.

TWENTY-SIX
VIX

I WHISTLED AS I STRAIGHTENED THE NEW AUTUMN display I'd put together the other day. I loved it here. Dasia and Yasmin were great employers. Both of them appreciated ideas from employees, and when I offered a suggestion for the display, they embraced it.

"I sold another of those scallop-necked tunics," Peyton, one of my new co-workers, said as she passed by. "And it was your display that caught her eye."

Pleased, I thanked her.

Work wasn't the only reason I had a spring in my step and a smile on my face.

Three days ago, waking up next to Carson, I'd worried things would be weird like before, but it was comfortable to shower and eat breakfast in his kitchen.

He told me he was leaving later that morning for San Ramon, California. Who could blame him for wanting a break? He'd worked like a dog over the last few weeks. He said he was eager to spend time with his parents, and suddenly I felt a flare of jealousy, envying the familial closeness I never had.

Still, that moment didn't ruin how good things were between us. Though I hadn't seen Carson since then, we talked and texted, even today. And we made plans to go out on Friday evening. Maybe it was too soon to hope for more, but for once, I wanted something more with a lover than just sex.

The thought that he might feel the same way left me equal parts excited and nervous.

Okay, more nervous than excited. I didn't know how this would work. I didn't have any relationships from my past—nothing more than a few casual dates, anyway—but I didn't have any examples of good relationships to look at.

How could I be with someone for real if I didn't know what *real* was?

That was the million-dollar question. But if Carson were half the man I knew him to be, we would figure it out together.

"Hey, Vix, I'm going on my break," Peyton called. "Back in fifteen."

I waved at her to let her know I heard and turned to the spreadsheet I was working on. Dasia and Yasmin said they would promote someone to manager soon, and it might be a good idea to do something extra to show I could handle the position if I applied.

The bell over the door rang, and I quickly saved my work before coming around the counter to greet the new customer.

Shock froze me in place as my brother walked toward me.

Wulf Silvers. We didn't look like siblings. He took more after his mother and me after mine. Even though he was ten years older, I was a few inches taller and a lot heavier. He always looked like he skipped half his meals, though my memories said he had a hearty appetite. His brown hair was longer than the last time I saw him, and it looked like he hadn't shaved in a couple of days. The light blue eyes and hooked nose were the same, though.

"You're difficult to track down, Vixen."

"I've gone by Vix since I was twelve," I reminded him. The response was automatic, and it broke me free of my stupor.

"You'd think with such a unique name, it'd be easy to find you." He stopped a couple of feet from me and stuck his hands in his pockets to signal he wasn't expecting a handshake or hug in greeting, which surprised me. The commune encouraged physical closeness, even beyond the sexual.

"I wasn't trying to hide," I said. That was mostly true.

"No?" He tried to raise one of his eyebrows, but he never mastered that gesture and only ended up with both eyebrows high, making him look surprised.

"How did you find me?" I asked, hoping I merely sounded curious rather than concerned. Now that my mind was working again, I could think of only one reason my brother would be here, and it wasn't good.

"You're famous," he said. "It's not like we're cut off from the world back home. You had to know your new occupation would put you front and center."

My new occupation?

Shit.

"The fashion show."

"I never realized you wanted to be a model," Wulf said, an edge to his tone that made his attempt at casualness a clear lie. "If I had to guess, I would've thought maybe a vet. You always liked animals. Though I guess if you were going to go to school, you would've done it right after getting your GED like Honey."

"We both know I didn't leave for a career," I said. "And modeling was just to earn some money while I was between jobs."

He looked around the store. "So you're doing what? Sales?"

I couldn't handle the small talk anymore. "You didn't come here to catch up. Did something happen to my sisters?"

Wulf shook his head. "They're fine. You know why I'm here."

I did, but I would make him say it.

"It's time for you to come home, Vixen." He took his hands out of his pockets and crossed his arms. "And I'm here to make sure you do."

"I am home, Wulf," I said, mimicking his stance. "I'm an adult, and it's my decision."

"You belong at the commune," he said, a stubborn

set to his jaw. "You're done fucking around here. You have responsibilities."

"Responsibilities?" I fought to keep my emotions under control. *"That's* what you're calling it?"

Color flooded his cheeks, but he didn't back down. "You have until Sunday to get your affairs in order, and then you're coming back with me. End of discussion."

Before I could even process such a ludicrous statement, he was out of the shop, and I was alone.

What the hell just happened?

And what the hell was I going to do about it?

TWENTY-SEVEN
CARSON

As much as New York was home, and I loved it, there was something to say about returning to San Ramon. My parents lived in the same massive house from my childhood, and although we were all grown, they'd kept our bedrooms the same.

At the moment, the only sibling who still lived with Mom and Da was Paris, and she was off on an archeological dig somewhere. Having my parents to myself wasn't something I got to experience often with a family as big as mine, and after the last few busy weeks, the quiet was welcome.

The next day, I was on my way to Palo Alto to see my twin brother, Cory. He was a bit of a workaholic, so I appreciated him taking time for a late lunch at Reposado Restaurant.

We weren't identical. Cory's hair was more reddish-brown than copper, and none of my curls, and his eyes were a pale green rather than blue. Yet, our features were similar enough that we could fool people about who was who growing up.

"The drive wasn't too bad?" he asked as we went inside.

"Not at all," I said and asked about our cousin. "Did Fury hassle you about taking a long lunch?"

Cory shook his head. "Fury is so absorbed in this new project, I think he's been sleeping at the office."

"It wouldn't be the first time," I said.

"No, it would not," he agreed.

We made small talk as we browsed the menus and placed our orders, catching up on everything in our lives. Cory congratulated me on my show.

"You outdid yourself this time," Cory said as he scooped salsa on a chip. "I caught a repeat of the live stream. Your models were amazing. That tall blonde is new, isn't she? What's her name?"

"Vix," I said shortly. "Her name's Vixen Teal."

Our waitress appeared. A drop-dead gorgeous brunette who made it difficult for my brother to order. He just said, 'I'll have what he's having' before I even said a word, so I ordered for both of us.

I caught him watching her leave but didn't comment on it. It was difficult for Cory to talk to strangers, especially women. The anxiety had been pretty bad when we were kids, but he came somewhat out of his shell when we hit high school.

"Tell me about your new model, Vixen Teal."

"Why so interested all of a sudden?"

He grinned. "Let's just say rumors are going

around."

Cory gave me a searching look.

"There is?" I asked. "What rumors?"

"London said you couldn't take your eyes off her during the after-party," he said. "Enough beating around the bush. Spill."

Cory knew me too well. It's difficult to hide stuff from your twin.

"Well," I began, "like I said, her name's Vix. And we met in a rather unusual way."

Cory listened as I told him everything. I didn't get into details of certain things, but enough that he knew Vix was more than a casual fling.

I didn't know what to call this thing between us, but I knew what it *wasn't*.

"And now we're going out on Friday," I concluded. "Our first proper date."

Cory said nothing for a while. I finished my meal and wondered what sort of insight I'd be getting from my trusted brother.

"I've got nothing."

I glared at him. "Asshat."

He laughed. "Seriously, Carson. It sounds like you know how much you like this woman. You just have to be honest with yourself...and with her."

I threw my straw wrapper at him. "That's not *nothing*."

He shrugged. "You would've figured it out on your own." He threw the wrapper back. "Maybe. You're not always the quickest on the uptake."

"She's unlike anyone I've ever met before," I said with a sigh. "I mean, she's gorgeous, but I've been around many people you could say that about. It's all the other things about her. From talking to her, watching her, interacting with her. She's amazing."

"You're worried you're not good enough," Cory said, understanding dawning on his face. "You think she's too good for you."

"She's a hell of a woman," I said. "She's too good for anyone."

"Does she think that too?" he asked.

"No," I said. "Vix is such an independent person. She doesn't expect anything from anybody, much less believe she's too good for anyone."

"I've heard about women like that," he said with a grin. "I never imagined they were real."

"Vix is real." I laughed. "She's always thinking of other people before she thinks of herself. I once saw her spend money she'd set aside for a new pair of sandals to buy some half-dead flowers from a pregnant panhandler."

"That was nice of her. She sounds great," he said and leaned back. "But don't sell yourself short."

"I'm not–" I protested.

"You are," he interrupted. "You always have. But everything you've said about Vix sounds like you two are meant for each other."

I leaned back and took another sip of my drink. "Maybe. I hope you're right."

TWENTY-EIGHT
VIX

WITH MIXED FEELINGS, I'D AGREED TO HAVE MY brother, Wulf, over for dinner. It was bound to be stressful, but it'd been two years since I'd seen anyone from the commune, and to be honest, I was curious about everything there.

But most of all, I wanted to settle our situation tonight. That way, I could focus on my date tomorrow evening and enjoy being with Carson again.

I checked the lasagna, and as I straightened, I heard the buzzer from the garage door entrance. I pressed the intercom.

"Hello?"

"Vixen, it's me."

I pressed the release button and swallowed a reminder about my name. He simply refused to call me Vix. "Come through the garage and up the stairs. My door is the one on the right."

I closed my eyes and breathed deeply as I waited,

trying to calm my nerves as my anxiety spiked. I never thought my brother could trigger my emotions like this again.

He knocked, and I put a smile on my face before opening the door.

"Hi. Come in."

"Hey." He stepped inside, eyes darting around the apartment.

I could imagine the things going through his brain right now. The commune where we grew up wasn't some backwoods thing with no electricity or heat. We had all the necessities. My apartment with Susanna hadn't been a shock to me, and it wouldn't have been to Wulf. But the luxury of this apartment took a bit of adjustment.

"That modeling job must've paid really well for you to afford this place," he said. His voice, like his expression, was bland and impossible to read.

"It's a recent thing," I said. "I got a good deal on it."

"Mm-hm."

I gestured toward the open space of the living room/dining room. "Have a seat. Can I get you something to drink?" I asked. "Juice, soda, water...wine?"

"Water's fine," he said. "As long as it's not bottled. You haven't gone that far, have you?"

I could feel my smile taking on a pinched look. "It's filtered but not bottled. Just because I left doesn't mean I condone wastefulness."

"Yeah, right." Wulf didn't bother hiding his skepticism.

Ignoring yet another needling remark, I went to the kitchen for the drinks and came back to find Wulf sitting at the dining table, back ramrod straight, hands lying flat on the table in a highly awkward position. He had never been comfortable in his own skin.

"I have a vegetarian lasagna in the oven," I said. "I remember you liked it."

"I do, thank you." He looked startled by my statement, a strangely vulnerable look flitting across his eyes.

"We didn't talk much the other day," I said after a moment of silence. "How's Oberlain?" A thought occurred to me. "Unless he changed his name again."

"Hmm?" Wulf blinked and turned his gaze to me as if his mind had been somewhere else. "No, our dad is still Oberlain. He's the same as always."

Our dad had been born Owen Chambers. He went by Oberlain Green, changing his name when joining the commune. A few people changed their names multiple times. And yet some couldn't be bothered to remember I preferred Vix over Vixen.

"And Phina?"

"She's good." Wulf smiled. That didn't surprise me. She wasn't his mother, but everyone liked her. "The gardens are doing well, and she's getting ready for the final harvesting."

"And Andrea?" My heart twisted at the thought of my brother's daughter. She was only nine when I left. She would have changed the most. "How is she?"

His smile widened, his eyes shining. "She's

wonderful. Top of her classes in everything except penmanship."

"She still has that messy handwriting?" I chuckled.

"Oh yes, she's looking forward to online classes next year because her handwriting won't be an issue, then."

"She's going to start online classes already?"

Some of the light went out of Wulf's smile. "That's what we're hoping for."

Alarm bells went off. "Is something wrong?"

He shook his head. "Lasagna smells like it's done."

He avoided answering my question, but he was right about the lasagna. My mind raced as I went to the kitchen. What was he hiding?

Wulf's expression was casual when I came back with the lasagna, but the light I had seen when he talked about his daughter was gone.

We filled our plates and ate in silence.

I looked harder at my older brother. He was wearing the same clothes he had on Tuesday, and they were wrinkled, though not dirty. But the closer I looked, the more I saw. His hair was greasy, like it'd been a while since he washed it. He had dirt under his fingernails, too.

"Where have you been staying?"

Wulf glanced at me as if confused by my question. "In the van."

"Oh, well, you can use my shower after eating." I made the offer nonchalantly, not wanting to wound his pride.

After a moment, he nodded. "I will. Thanks." He put down his fork. "But we need to talk about when we're leaving."

Dammit.

I knew this was coming, but a part of me hoped he'd see I had a life here and let the matter drop.

"I'm not going back, Wulf," I said, keeping my voice as firm as possible without sounding annoyed. "I have a job here. Friends." Maybe more than friends, but I didn't give voice to that thought.

He scowled. "Pyxis wants you back, Vixen."

I felt like he threw a bucket of ice water on me. I suspected Wulf's sudden appearance in New York wasn't because he missed me. He came for the same reason he did anything. Because Pyxis Machoi told him to.

"It doesn't matter what he wants," I said tightly. "I'm an adult, and it's my decision."

Wulf's jaw clenched, tension radiating from him. "You have to come back."

"No, I don't." I could probably count on one hand the number of times in my life I lost my temper. However, if Wulf didn't let this go, this would be one of them.

"Don't you want to see everyone?" he asked. "Andrea and Zhora? You cared about them. At least, you used to."

"I still do," I said. "Very much."

The thought of my niece and my best friend made

my heartache. Since I left, I hadn't spoken to either of them, and I missed them so badly it hurt.

"Andrea cried for days when she found out you were gone."

I glared at my brother. "That's a low blow. You know why I left."

"And that's exactly why you have to come back," he said. "Pyxis will not let you continue like this. If you don't come back with me, he'll send someone else."

The words chilled me to the bone.

He'll send someone else.

"It's been two years," I said. "Surely, he has plenty of women who are more than willing to go to bed with him."

Something dark passed through Wulf's eyes, and my stomach clenched. I didn't know what it meant, but my gut said it wasn't anything good.

"It doesn't matter," he said. "He wants you, and he's determined to have you."

"You're right. It doesn't matter because he can't have me. The only person who owns me is me."

Wulf stared at me in disbelief, then changed the subject. "You mentioned a shower. Does that offer still stand?"

"Of course," I said. "Let me get you some towels."

After getting him situated in the guest bathroom, a turmoil of emotions swirled through me, and memories of my past life flooded in.

A peaceful childhood.

A tyrant.

A man who made me feel things I had never felt before.

Friends, old and new.

Running through rows of corn, bare feet in the dirt.

The sounds of half a dozen others sleeping around me.

Fear.

Peace.

Anger.

Love.

Frustration.

I had no intention of ever going back, but I wasn't foolish enough to think Wulf would give up. He said he would give me until Sunday, and I had a feeling he wouldn't stop asking until then.

If at all.

I washed the dishes, and as I set the last plate into the rack, I heard the bathroom door open.

"Thanks," he said as he came into the room.

"You're welcome." Yeah, this wasn't awkward at all. "Let me walk you down."

"No, thanks." He shook his head. "I remember the way. And I think you need some time to think."

"Wulf..." I began.

He made a sharp gesture with his hand. "You know what you have to do, Vixen. I'll be in touch again. Get your head screwed on straight before then."

I didn't respond as I followed him out the door. I watched him go down the stairs before shutting my eyes and resting my forehead against the wood.

Dammit.

Needing to unwind, I headed to the bathroom and filled the tub.

Ten minutes later, I sank under the vanilla-scented bubbles and let out a sigh. The porcelain was cool on my bare neck with my hair twisted up, but the water was hot. As I leaned back and closed my eyes, I could finally let my thoughts out of their mental box.

Two years ago, I walked away from everything and everyone I knew.

The commune was for people who wanted to have an elite community. Decisions were made by group consensus. Everyone worked, and everyone had a vote. It was a great system.

But all that changed when *he* arrived. An outsider.

I was eighteen when Pyxis Machoi, a handsome man with degrees in psychology and social work, asked to move into the commune. Everyone thought he would be a brilliant addition, and with his pitch-black hair and azure eyes combined with electric charisma, he made all the women swoon.

Except me.

I never returned his interest. Not that it seemed to matter to him. From that first moment, he pursued me. For six months, he took my refusals with smiles that didn't quite reach his eyes but no insults or threats. He didn't even apply any extra pressure or persuasion.

And then everything changed. For everyone.

Six weeks.

A DRESS FOR CURVES

That's how long it took to go from status quo to shocking.

Little by little, he manipulated everybody, and by using his charm, mixed with his flair for politics, he soon had more followers than detractors.

They declared him the new leader at the next assembly with an overwhelming majority. After that, it didn't take long for new rules to be imposed. There was nothing major initially, but less than two months after he took over, he called everyone into an assembly and announced that all the women in the commune now belonged to him. While he insisted he wouldn't force any of us, he 'encouraged' us not to refuse him.

The announcement had come as a shock, but it did not surprise me when he approached me right away. He made his 'offer' as if it was some sort of privilege, a gift. When I told him no, his expression made me wonder if I really had a choice.

I tried to convince the others to revolt, take our power back, and kick Pyxis out. No one listened to me. They insisted he was protecting us. It was an honor to be chosen by him, but if we didn't want to, he wouldn't force the issue.

During the next couple of months, it seemed like he honored his statement that he wouldn't force sex. But, as his demands became more forceful, his 'hints' more direct, I made my choice.

And here I was.

In a hot bubble bath, trying to figure out how to

convince my brother I wouldn't be returning to that place and that man.

As I dried off, my phone buzzed, distracting me. The text from Carson was simple enough, saying he was back home and that he would see me tomorrow for our date.

That was enough to give my mind a safe place to focus, a respite from these other thoughts.

My date with a gorgeous man I longed to see again.

TWENTY-NINE
CARSON

I LOVED SPENDING TIME WITH MY PARENTS, AND visiting California was always a pleasant break from reality, but I enjoyed my work, and returning home never felt like a burden. However, returning to New York wasn't merely about being refreshed and ready to jump into my routine this time.

I wanted to see Vix.

I missed her. The way her smile lit up everything. How her eyes changed shades depending on her mood, ranging from a pale violet that was almost blue to a deep, near-purple. That last one was my favorite because it was her eyes' color when she was aroused.

By the time the plane landed in New York, I had decided to stop by my studio to pick up the mail. It wasn't too late for me to go through it when I got home...or to check in on Vix. If she were home, maybe she'd want to chat.When I got to my studio, I handed the driver a fifty-dollar tip. "Wait here. If I'm not back in ten minutes, you can leave. I'm surprising someone."

"No problem." He grinned at me.

Practically whistling, I unlocked the studio door and went inside. Impatient, I didn't bother looking at the mail and continued to the back entrance through the building.

I had just opened the door when I saw the doors opening into the garage. My pulse kicked up in anticipation, and I opened my mouth to call out a greeting when someone, who was definitely *not* Vix, came out of the garage.

As the figure came out of a shadow, I saw scruff on his face, brown hair, and a hooked nose.

His hair was wet like he'd just showered.

I closed the door and sank against the wall, my mind racing.

There was only one possibility.

He was someone Vix had invited over.

And he'd used her shower.

I pushed all thoughts aside and hurried out to the car that was, fortunately, still waiting.

"Your girl is not home?" the driver asked as I got into the car.

"No." I gave him a forced smile. "It's home for me then."

I rattled off my address and then sat in silence as we drove.

Entering the lobby, the desk clerk waved and welcomed me back, but I didn't stop to chat.

When I got to the apartment, I went through the motions of putting away my things before ordering food. Only when I'd finished eating did I examine my feelings.

Jealousy. That was a given. I practically bit my twin's head off when he said she was attractive. A week after we had amazing sex, she slept with someone else. Jealousy wasn't surprising at all.

And anger went with it. At her. At myself.

I pushed the remains of my Chinese takeout rice around on my plate as I thought. Vix and I never defined anything. We didn't put a label or name to what we were. We never discussed exclusivity. We barely knew each other, and it wasn't as if we followed a traditional path, either. We didn't meet, go out, kiss, sleep together, and along the way, figure things out. I couldn't even say if she was on the same page as me.

I hadn't even known what page I was on until I'd talked to Cory. Or, at least, I hadn't admitted it to myself.

Even if she had slept with the guy I saw, unless she was in love with him, I didn't care. I needed to know if she wanted me as much as I wanted her.

I scraped my plate into the trash and dumped the food's packaging. Then I sent Vix a text, letting her know I was home and that I'd see her tomorrow evening.

But how would I make it through the next twenty-some hours without going crazy?

THIRTY
CARSON

Today sucked.

Vix was working at the boutique, and I had nothing to do. Usually, that would've been my cue to go back to work, but I wasn't ready to go into the studio yet. I could work from home, but at this rate, with my mind still churning over that guy I saw, it would take most of the day just to get through the mail.

By the time I was ready for a shower, it felt like I'd spent the entire day beating my head against a wall for all I'd accomplished. I kept going round and round in my mind, wondering if Vix felt the same way as I felt about her.

Leopard at des Artistes was the kind of place where a suit was appropriate, and since I planned to have a serious conversation with Vix, looking my best was a good idea. I selected my favorite black suit I designed last year. Maybe I could score a few points in my favor for being a snappy dresser.

It seemed to work. When Vix opened the door to her apartment, her expression told me so. Her eyes glowed as her gaze ran down my body and up again, tempting me to fuck her right now. But we had to do things right if this relationship would be more than just a fling. We needed to discuss our feelings and where we wanted things to go. Being vulnerable wasn't easy for me. Opening up always meant a chance to get hurt.

But *damn,* she was smoking hot.

She wore the little black dress I designed for the fashion show, sexy and appropriate for fine dining.

"You look amazing," I said.

"Well, the dress *was* made for me," she said. "By an amazing and talented guy. He's pretty good-looking too."

"Oh, really?" I teased. "Maybe you should go out with him tonight instead."

Vix laughed and said she was ready to go.

AS SOON AS we placed our orders, Vix fixed me with a serious look and asked what was wrong.

"Nothing's wrong," I said.

She raised an eyebrow.

"I just want to talk to you about something, and I've been trying to figure out the best way to approach it."

"I always appreciate straightforward," she said with a smile.

"All right then." I took a deep breath. "I want us to be exclusive."

She stared at me.

"We haven't talked about what we are to each other," I continued. "And while I know what I want, I don't know what you—"

"What do you mean you want to be exclusive?"

My heart sank. "I mean...I don't want to see anyone else, and I was hoping you didn't either. I know that's not how you were raised–"

She held up a hand, a confused expression on her face. "I thought we already were exclusive."

"I thought so, too." I chose my next words carefully. "But I stopped by the studio on my way home from the airport last night and saw a guy coming out of the garage and didn't want to make any assumptions...."

One corner of her mouth tipped up, and her eyes twinkled. "That was my brother, Wulf."

"Your brother?" I let my relief show on my face. Honesty and straightforwardness were working pretty well so far.

"Shocked the hell out of me," she said with a laugh. "He just showed up at work on Tuesday."

"Tuesday?" It surprised me she hadn't told me before and it kind of hurt that she hadn't.

"I was going to tell you." She reached for my hand. "I wasn't hiding it. Just...figuring it out."

"Figuring out what?" I asked, sensing it was something more than a surprise visit.

"Why he showed up." She made a dismissive

gesture with a casualness I didn't quite believe. "But not now. Let's talk about something else."

"No problem. We can talk about whatever you want." I was obviously curious why his visit bothered her, but I'd let her decide if or when that discussion happened.

We paused as the waiter returned with our food and began eating. For a while, we made small talk before Vix brought the conversation back to what I had started.

"Can I ask, did you only want to talk about exclusivity because you thought I slept with someone else?" Vix sounded genuinely curious.

"No. It was my brother Cory's suggestion." I decided to come clean. "When I was visiting my family in California, I talked with him."

"About me?" she asked.

I nodded, reached out, and put my hand on hers, my fingers tracing patterns on her skin. "And Cory did what he always does...helped me understand what's going on in my head."

"And what's that?" she asked.

"I want a relationship with you." That was easier to say than I thought. "I don't have much experience, and I might even suck at it, but I want to try."

She smiled at me, her eyes shining. "I'd like that too. And I'm also a beginner at relationships."

"Do you think it would work?" I asked.

"There's only one way to find out," she said.

The waiter returned, and the anxiety I'd felt all

day disappeared. After resolving the questions that had bothered me for the past week, I could breathe again. Vix looked as if she felt the same, and our conversation drifted to lighter topics.

As we finished our dessert, the immediate future had precedence over both of our minds. I couldn't wait to get Vix in my arms and kiss her luscious lips. And with only a couple of words, we went back to her place to continue our date. I needed to fuck her, make love to her. A week was much too long to go without having her.

THIRTY-ONE
VIX

It was the perfect date. I loved how Carson opened up to me, and no matter how innocent, every time he touched me, my pulse raced, and heat flooded my cheeks.

After the waiter brought the check, I asked if he wanted to come to my place for the night. His expression made it obvious we felt the same. Not just the heat of arousal, but one of a deeper kind of affection.

He couldn't keep his hands off me as we waited for his car to be brought around, and after that, he drove with one hand, the other linked with mine. The absent back-and-forth movements of his thumb on my skin made every cell in my body light up. It was such a small, innocent gesture. It took everything I had not to tell him to pull over so I could have him right there.

It must've shown on my face. When Carson glanced at me, his eyes heated. I pressed my thighs together as if that could do me any real good. Only one thing could fix the deep ache inside me.

"What's going on in that head of yours?" he asked, his voice low.

I didn't know whether I was trying to shock him or be honest. "I'm trying to figure out how to keep myself under control when all I want to do is jump you at the next red light."

"Fuck, Vix," he growled. "What am I supposed to do with that?"

A bit of wickedness came over me, and I went with it. "Well, you could help a girl out."

He raised an eyebrow. "And what does that mean?"

As he came to a stop at a light, I spread my legs, the movement raising my skirt until I nearly flashed my panties. I guided his hand under my skirt without a word until his fingertips brushed damp fabric.

"Vix."

I wasn't sure if my name was a warning or a plea. I rocked against his hand, and he cursed. Somehow, still paying attention to the light, he slipped his fingers beneath my panties and between my folds.

He groaned. "Damn, baby, you're so wet."

With his fingers teasing my clit, I could only whimper in response, but that was enough to earn a chuckle. He slid a finger inside me, and my head fell back against the seat. The car windows were lightly tinted, and it would've been difficult for anyone to see inside at this time of night. Still, as Carson continued, the nearly public nature of the situation had adrenaline buzzing through me. Disproving the idea that men couldn't multi-task, Carson added a second finger and found a steady rhythm that he kept up while driving us back to my place.

"Don't come just yet," he cautioned. "I want to look at you when you do."

I tried to glare at him, but couldn't do anything other than gasp and moan. I reached the point where I was shamelessly moving against his hand, desperate to reach that peak, but his words had me fighting back my pleasure, my desire to please him greater than my need for release. My hands curled into fists at my sides, and my body tensed, hovering on the edge.

"I can't, I can't..."

The car came to a jerking stop in the garage. "Come for me, Vix. Now. Come for me."

I let go and cried out as my orgasm burst over and through me. His fingers lightly stroked me, drawing it out until I finally collapsed, limp. In a daze, I opened my eyes to see him licking his fingers clean, and a shudder went through me.

So. Fucking. Hot.

"That was—"

Before he could get the rest of his sentence out, I grabbed the front of his shirt and crushed my lips against his. The taste of chocolate, wine, and *me* made my head spin. He cupped the back of my head as his tongue plundered my mouth, and I felt the embers of arousal flame to life again. It wasn't my turn, though.

I dropped my hand to his lap and found him already hard. He groaned as I massaged him through his pants, then tore his mouth away. "Upstairs."

"Not yet." I gave him my best seductive smile and shifted into a better position. Confused, he stared at me until I unzipped his pants and reached inside, fingers wrapping around the thick, hot flesh I found.

"Vix, you don't—"

"Let me do this." I slid my hand up and down the silky soft skin, keeping the pressure light. I could spend hours exploring his body, touching every inch of him, but I would get him off fast and dirty now. We could take our time later. I met his eyes and said, "Don't hold back."

With that, I lowered my head. He cursed as I fastened my lips around the tip, and I smiled for a moment before applying all of my focus to my goal. Keeping one hand around the base, I took as much of him as possible. Using suction and just the slightest hint of teeth, I found a rhythm that had him cursing and groaning. Every sound he made tightened my stomach, turning me on even further, and I was tempted to slide a hand into my panties and get myself off again.

"Vix, baby..." His voice was hoarse, with the same rough sound he had before he came.

I squeezed him lightly and sucked harder, signaling that I meant what I said, not to hold back. I wanted him to come in my mouth, wanted his taste to coat my tongue. I didn't always like it, but I wanted that connection with him. I wanted the intimacy that could come from that sort of interaction. An intimacy I now knew was possible between the two of us.

The barest touch of teeth was the last bit he needed before he shouted my name, and his body tensed. A moment later, his cock twitched and pulsed, flooding my mouth with his cum.

When I raised my head after I'd swallowed the last drop, I found Carson staring down at me, his eyes the most blazing blue I'd ever seen. I opened my mouth to say something, only to have him grab me and haul me up against him. The kiss scorched me, set every inch of me on fire. Where he touched me, I burned, and the sounds he made told me he did as well.

When the need for air finally made us pull apart, we were both flushed and panting; our bodies wound tight once again, and our appetite for each other whetted rather than sated.

"Upstairs?" he asked.

I nodded. "I want a bed for the next round so we can take our time."

His lips curved into a smile that sent a shiver up my spine. "I like the sound of that."

We held hands in the elevator, letting the fire between us simmer, but the electricity hadn't dissipated by the time we entered the apartment. It still crackled as we took off our shoes and moved toward the bedroom, shedding our clothes along the way. As I stopped at the edge of the bed and turned to face him, I took a moment to appreciate the view.

He truly was a beautiful man. Long, lean lines and cut muscles. That trail of dark curls, glimmering bronze in the dim light. The deep v-grooves that I planned to lick at some point tonight. And that long, thick, beautiful cock was already starting to perk up again.

"Sit down," he said, gesturing toward the bed. "I only had a little taste before. I want a better one now."

Happy to comply, I sat on the edge of the bed and leaned back on my elbows so I could watch.

He went to his knees in front of me and pushed my legs apart. A kiss to the inside of my thigh sent goosebumps breaking out across my skin. He kissed his way up, parted lips and a touch of the tongue, each point of connection a spark that paled in comparison to the anticipation of what was to come. And then he was where I wanted him to be, his tongue playing where his fingers had been not too long ago.

Soft and wet, the muscle moved over every inch of sensitive skin, over and between my folds, tracing my entrance and then circling my clit. Each pass sent a ripple of pleasure across my nerves, building the pressure inside me a little higher. He didn't rush. He was single-minded in his focus, and I gave myself over to his care.

I floated. Flew. Rode the waves as they came and crested. With each one, the pleasure grew until I exploded, spots dancing behind my eyelids. I cried out his name, my hands reaching, clutching until his hand found mine. He laced his fingers between mine, and I clung to him, using him as a tether as I returned to myself.

A movement made me open my eyes, and I found Carson standing now, his free hand wrapped around his cock, leisurely stroking up and down the swollen shaft. His heated gaze moved up my body to meet my eyes.

"Are you ready for more?"

I pushed myself up the bed until I could stretch out completely. Once settled, I held out my hand.

"I'm ready. Are you?"

"Sweetheart, I've been dying to get inside you all night." He rolled on a condom and climbed onto the bed. "Please tell me you will not make me wait any longer."

I shook my head, and that was all he needed to press me down into the mattress. I welcomed the weight of him as I wrapped my legs around his waist. He slid home with one smooth stroke as our bodies came together. We were made for each other.

As we made love, I let the truth of that phrase permeate every inch of me. I knew reality would come in, and maybe it would show that we were too different to make things work, but right now, as we moved together, I set aside thoughts of the future and focused on the present. We could deal with everything else when it came.

"Fuck, sweetheart, you feel so good." He kissed the side of my neck. "Never want to stop. Want this forever."

Emotion merged with sensations threatening to overwhelm me, and I dug my nails into his shoulders. Growling, he bit down on my neck, sending a thrill of pain shooting down my nerves. I gasped, arching up against him, and the position put the right combination of friction and pressure on my clit to push me over the edge. As my body tightened around him, he let out a strangled cry, the sound muffled against my skin, and I felt him come.

The world dimmed around me until only Carson and I existed, bodies joined as closely as two people could be, sharing pleasure in a way that was beyond anything I had with anyone else. And I lost myself in him. In us.

Because I knew he'd find me.

THIRTY-TWO
CARSON

I lost count of the number of orgasms Vix had. After our first round on the bed, we fell asleep, but not for long. Then it was shower sex and collapsing in bed again for more.

I woke several hours later, spooning Vix. And with another hard-on.

I had one arm draped across her waist, and I slid it up to cup one heavy breast. The nipple pebbled against my palm, and I felt her breathing change as she stirred.

"Good morning," I murmured as I brushed my thumb back and forth over her nipple. "Sleep well?"

"Mmm..." She pushed her ass against my erection. "I did. You?"

"I'm enjoying waking up a lot more," I teased before pressing a kiss to her bare shoulder. "Any reason we have to rush out of bed?"

She reached back, her hand caressing my hip

before dropping between us to grip my cock. I groaned as her fingers wrapped around me and, for a moment, my brain short-circuited, making me forget my goal.

"Don't go back to sleep," she warned.

"No worries about that," I assured her. "I'm *very* awake."

"Good." She gave me a light squeeze before releasing me and leaning toward the bedside table. A moment later, she held up a condom packet.

I chuckled and kissed the side of her neck where I'd left a mark last night. I couldn't deny the possessiveness I felt when I saw it. "I like a woman who knows what she wants."

"I can't get enough of you," she said, reaching back to grab my ass. "All the time. Every time I'm anywhere near you, I want you."

"Does that mean you're ready for me?" I asked, slipping the tip of my middle finger between her folds to brush against her clit. "Are you nice and wet?"

She caught her breath when I touched that sensitive bundle of nerves, and I lightly stroked her for a few seconds before dropping my hand lower to slide my finger into her pussy.

"You are." I nipped her shoulder. "You're so fucking wet, baby."

She nodded, writhing as I pumped my finger in and out of her, keeping the heel of my hand pressed against her clit.

"I'm going to take you now," I said.

"Yes," she gasped. "Yes, please."

Then her nails dug deeper into my arm, and I was lost. I barely kept my fingers playing with her clit as I came, and the moment I felt her follow me, I let myself go completely.

When I came back to myself, she was limp in my arms, a satisfied smile on her face.

"Shower?"

I FINISHED SHOWERING before Vix and headed to the kitchen to scrounge up some breakfast. I found some instant oatmeal and popped it in the microwave.

I was just taking it out when a loud buzz made me jump. It took me a second to realize that it was the door. Vix had said nothing about expecting a visitor today, but I still pushed the intercom button.

"Hello?" I said.

"Who's this?"

An annoyed male voice made me bristle, but I kept my temper. My experience with Vix taught me how important it was not to jump to conclusions.

"Who are you looking for?" I asked.

"Vixen Teal. Who are you, and what are you doing in her apartment?"

I had a hunch who I was talking to. "I'm a friend of hers. Is she expecting you?"

"I'm her brother, and I want to talk to her. Let me up."

I wanted to tell him to fuck off, but I couldn't

decide for Vix. I would, however, be there to support her and back her up.

"Just a minute."

I went down the hall to her bedroom and then to the bathroom door. Not hearing the shower running, I knocked.

"Come in."

I opened the door to find Vix wearing only a towel wrapped around her as she braided her hair. Desire was like a punch to the gut, and I forgot for a moment why I was here.

"You okay?" she asked.

"I am." I smiled. "Your brother's downstairs and says he wants to talk to you. I didn't want to let him up without talking to you first."

Something flickered across her face, too fast for me to identify, and then she nodded. "Sure. Let him up, and I'll be out in a minute."

As I walked back down the hall, I was unsure if I should leave the apartment. I didn't want to intrude on a private matter, but Vix might need me.

"Come on up." I hit the button to unlock the door and then waited, surprised by how nervous I suddenly was. Despite whatever was going on between Vix and Wulf, he was still her brother, and I wanted to make a good impression. And for all I knew, he might be the only family of hers I'd ever meet.

When I opened the door, I recognized him clearly as the man I'd seen Thursday night. But I couldn't see any resemblance to Vix. None of her kindness and light, none of her sweetness or optimism.

"Come in," I said, stepping aside. "I'm Carson McCrae."

"And you're my sister's...what? Sugar daddy?" He gave me a scornful look as he came inside. "She said she got a good deal on this apartment. I'm guessing you keep it for your...*friends*."

I bit back a sharp reply and forced myself to be polite. "Yes, I own the apartment, but your sister is renting it from me the same way other tenants have in the past." Then, daring to make a slight presumption, I added, "I'm also her boyfriend."

"Funny." He smirked. "She didn't mention having a boyfriend before."

I felt my smile tighten, and I swallowed another smart comment. Fortunately, Vix appeared, or I might not have let his next snarky comment slide.

"Wulf, hey. I didn't realize you were stopping by today." She stepped up next to me and reached over to squeeze my hand. "Did you and Carson introduce yourselves?"

"We did," I said. I kissed her cheek. "I made oatmeal for breakfast. Maybe your brother would like to join us?"

"I've already eaten," Wulf said. "And we don't have time to fuck around, Vixen."

I clenched my jaw. Okay...this dirtbag just topped my list of first-rate assholes. But Vix wasn't weak. Unless Wulf crossed a serious line, I'd be her support rather than take away her control. If I learned anything from my sister, Maggie, sometimes a woman didn't need a white knight to save her. She needed one to stand at her side.

"Don't be a jerk," she said firmly. "You're a guest in my home."

"This isn't your home," he snapped. "You need to come home with me."

My eyebrows shot up. "She what?"

Vix released my hand and crossed her arms, a firm expression on her face. "We've talked about this already. More than once. I'm not going back."

That's why he was here? He was trying to get Vix to go back to the commune?

"I can't believe you're being so stubborn about this." He shook his head.

"And I can't believe that you, of all people, are pushing the subject."

There was an edge to her voice that I had never heard before, something almost... brittle.

"What's that supposed to mean?" Wulf's jaw jutted out. "'You of all people'?"

"You know exactly what I mean." Vix glanced at me for privacy, the gesture so slight I nearly missed it.

She didn't want me to know what they were discussing.

"I'll put the oatmeal away," I said and walked into the kitchen.

This was a family matter, and it didn't involve me. It wasn't like I had her coming to family events. Hell, she hadn't even met my siblings who lived here in the city. Our relationship was still brand new.

"Don't act like you don't know. You do."

She didn't lower her voice, which made me wonder if perhaps I was wrong about her not wanting me to know what was going on.

"No, Vixen, I don't."

Even without seeing his face, I knew he was lying.

"You know exactly why I left then and why I can't go back. Because of him."

I frowned as I put the oatmeal into the fridge. I could stay where I was, but my gut said something terrible was going on.

"I never understood why you freaked out about it," Wulf said sullenly. "Being chosen by him was an honor."

What the hell did *that* mean?

Vix didn't look my way as I returned to my spot next to her. I didn't say a word.

"An honor?" Vix shook her head in disbelief. "I know he's your friend and everyone back there worships the ground he walks on, but he's not a god, Wulf. He's not even a good person, yet you're still defending him."

"You don't know what's going on!" Wulf took a step toward her, and that was it.

I moved between them. "Back off."

"This isn't any of your business." Wulf glared up at me.

I couldn't decide if the bluster was stupidity or

arrogance. Vix could've outmatched him physically, but he was her brother, and I wasn't sure she'd hurt him, even if necessary. I didn't want her in a position where she had to make that choice.

"*She's* my business," I said.

Vix put a hand on my arm and moved, but kept me between them. I wasn't sure if she did it because she was scared of her brother or knew I wanted to be there. Whichever, he'd have to go through me first if he tried to get to her.

"You're so brainwashed you think this is okay," she said.

"I'm not the one who's been brainwashed," Wulf argued. "We all live there to avoid the poison our commercialized and corrupted society emits, and here you are, drowning in the middle of it, and you don't even realize it."

Vix frowned. "It's not like that."

"Really?" He gave me another disgusted look. "Then why, when I find you after two years, do you need to sell your body?"

"Excuse me?"

Wulf continued, "Parading around in front of people in those dresses is bad enough, but to be seen in your underwear, almost naked? And now I find out you're fucking some guy for this apartment? I never thought you'd stoop so low. You have no shame."

My hands curled into fists, and I opened my mouth to say something, but Vix beat me to it.

"First of all, I'm not sleeping with Carson because

he's renting me this apartment." Vix's face was flushed, but her tone was even. "And second, where is all this coming from? We were raised to celebrate and appreciate our bodies. We didn't shame others for their sexual choices, either. Even if I *was* selling sex to anyone, as long as it's consensual, it's no one's business but mine. Everything they taught us emphasized embracing the natural world, including our sexuality."

"And it was wrong." Wulf folded his arms, a mutinous expression on his face. "That sort of teaching ruined the world, and it was ruining our home."

"What are you talking about?" She took a step forward. "We had no problems until Pyxis showed up. We were free to be with who we wanted and to leave when we wanted."

"Maybe you were free to be with who you wanted, but not all of us were."

A lightbulb went off in my head. "You wanted someone who didn't want you."

Wulf's head snapped around, and he glared at me. "Shut the fuck up."

"Is that what this is about?" Vix asked. "I know when Apple left it was hard, but there were other women."

Wulf's neck reddened, and I said, "None of them wanted you, did they? You're being judgmental about your sister because you never got laid."

Color rushed into his face. "I'm being 'judgmental' because Vix is flaunting her body and fucking around when she belongs to someone else!"

My jaw dropped. Vix *belonged* to someone else? There was so much to unpack in those words that I didn't know where to start.

"I don't *belong* to that bastard!" Vix raised her voice louder than I'd heard before. "Pyxis may have shared his bed with all the other women, but I *never* agreed to it. He has no claim on me!"

Pyxis.

"What the hell was going on here? Who's Pyxis?" I said.

"Stay the fuck out of this," Wulf shouted, then pointed at Vix. "You've had your time away, and it's time to come back to him. He's waited long enough."

Things were clicking into place. I didn't have all the details, but enough to get the idea.

This Pyxis guy sent his friend, Vix's brother, to get her to come back and "marry" this nasty dude.

Like there was any universe in which I would let that happen.

THIRTY-THREE
VIX

"You mother-fucking bastard!" The words came out of Carson with a force that shocked me into taking a step back. He wasn't yelling, exactly, but the intensity radiating from him made this even more frightening.

"What kind of man would sell out his sister to be raped? Are you insane?"

"That's not what I'm doing," Wulf protested.

"No?" Carson took a step toward my brother. "This Pyxis piece-of-shit asshole wants Vix. And he told you to go get her so he could fuck her, didn't he?"

Wulf shook his head, but I could tell his heart wasn't in it.

"Forcing sex with someone who doesn't want it *is* the definition of rape."

"You don't get it," Wulf said. "Vix will be honored to be chosen by him and share his bed."

"Like hell, I will," I muttered. "I don't want Pyxis. I don't even *like* him."

"You heard her," Carson said. "She said no. That's that. Now, piss off!"

"No, it's not!" Wulf reached out a hand.

Carson moved before I could react, grabbing the front of Wulf's shirt and shoving him against the nearest wall. Wulf's eyes went wide with fear.

"I will *not* stand by and watch what happened to my sister happen to Vix," Carson snarled.

"What the fuck are you talking about? I've never touched your sister. I don't know her, man."

"She was a rape victim by an abusive boyfriend, just like Vix will become if she goes back." Carson let go of Wulf and stepped back, keeping himself between us. Still my protector.

"Carson's right," I said to Wulf. "Pyxis won't respect a refusal. If I went back with you, he'd take me, no matter what." Seeing the reluctance on my brother's face, I stated it more boldly. "He will rape me, Wulf."

"Why can't you just be like the rest of the girls?" Wulf hunched his shoulders, looking more like a child than an adult. "They don't have a problem sleeping with him."

"You never got it," I told my brother. "Everyone thought Pyxis was charismatic and wonderful, but I despised him. I would never say yes."

"But you have to."

I was done with this back and forth. "What's going on, Wulf?" I asked. "Why are you so insistent I go?"

"Please. Just believe me when I say you need to come back." Frustration bled through his voice as his eyes met mine.

"Just fucking tell us," Carson said. "Tell us what's so important?"

"It's none of your business!" Wulf practically shouted at him. "It's about family, and you're not family!"

"Dammit, Wulf!" I snapped. "Tell me or leave and never come back!"

He stared at me as if he couldn't believe what I said, and then he crumpled. He let out a choked sob and pressed the heels of his hands to his eyes.

Despite everything, I went to Wulf. Putting my arm around him, I led him to the couch and sat next to him as he struggled to get control. The knot in my stomach tightened. Possibilities raced through my mind.

"He lied." Wulf finally got the words out.

"What?"

"Pyxis. He lied to us." Wulf looked up, anguish in his pale blue eyes.

This wasn't an act. I could see the pain, and my stomach clenched.

"He—he decided that, on the Autumn Equinox, he will claim all women who have...come of age." He looked sick.

Carson was the one who asked. "What, exactly, does that mean?"

"Once a girl menstruates." The words were barely

a whisper. "The next equinox or solstice, he'll claim her." Then my brother looked at me with eyes full of helplessness and desperation. "Andrea had her first period three weeks ago."

All the strength ran out of my legs, and I was grateful I was already sitting. I could feel the blood draining from my face.

"Andrea?" Carson looked at Wulf. "That's your daughter, isn't it?"

He nodded. "She's eleven."

Carson uttered a string of obscenities that I wholeheartedly agreed with.

Pyxis was a slimy bastard. I always suspected he was a rapist, but never this.

"He announced it on the Summer Solstice," Wulf continued.

"This guy is a bloody creep," Carson said.

"Then, about a week ago, he came to me." Wulf took a deep breath and let it out slowly. "He promised to leave Andrea alone if I could get you to come home."

The realization struck me like a blow to the chest. My brother was here to save his daughter, and I was the one who could do it.

Fuck. Now what do I do?

THIRTY-FOUR
CARSON

Wulf wasn't trying to hurt Vix. He might not have gone about it the most intelligent way, but he was trying to save his daughter.

All of my anger shifted to the real villain, Pyxis Machoi.

That man had driven Vix from her home and threatened her. He threatened her niece. Hell, he threatened all the females in the entire commune.

I wasn't a violent person. I was more likely to deflect with charm and humor than push back in a conflict, but I wouldn't pass up an opportunity to knock out a few of Pyxis's teeth if the chance presented itself. However, I couldn't let emotions control my actions. We had to act smart about this.

"I'll get Louis on the case," I said. "He has a direct line to the DA's assistant. Don't ask me how."

Vix gave me a puzzled look. "I'm pretty sure the

commune isn't under the jurisdiction of any New York City precinct."

I frowned. "Right. But they can contact the right people. Maybe the FBI will need to be involved."

Wulf shook his head. "It won't do any good. Pyxis will just convince everyone to say that nothing illegal is happening. Even if I tell the truth, they'll say that I misunderstood or am lying."

"And you believe these people will defend a man who plans to rape their daughters? Why didn't you take your daughter and leave?"

"I couldn't." Wulf tugged at his hair. "None of us can."

"What do you mean you can't leave?" Vix asked, her eyes wide.

"That fence around the compound that he started building before you left," Wulf said. "He finished it. That's not all. Shortly after you left, Pyxis brought in some old friends. His buddies, he called them. There are five of them, and they have guns." Wulf raised his head. "'For our protection', Pyxis said, and we went along with him. Now, we're no longer allowed to leave the commune."

"You left," I pointed out.

"He sent me here because he knew I wouldn't risk anything with my daughter there," Wulf shot back. "Only his selected few can go in or out."

"All right," I said. "This actually makes things easier. That's kidnapping and illegal detainment. The FBI will definitely get involved now."

"Do you think so?" Vix asked, a flicker of hope in her eyes. "I mean, can we just walk into the FBI and get them to listen to us?"

"I'm not sure how it works, but keeping people captive is a big deal."

"I don't have the time to wait for you to convince the FBI to look into a commune," Wulf said, his voice flat and his shoulders slumped. "It could take weeks to get them to listen."

"What's the hurry?" Vix asked.

"When Pyxis sent me after you, he said I need to be back before the equinox."

"Which is Tuesday," she said. "Today is Saturday."

"This morning, I got a call from my daughter."

My stomach roiled.

"She was so excited because Pyxis had told her she would have a special part in the ceremony on Tuesday. Pyxis had also told her he would decide tomorrow what that special part entailed." Wulf looked straight at Vix. "If I don't bring you back by tomorrow, he'll select Andrea."

"If we tell the FBI everything you told us, they'll get all the kids out, including your daughter," I said.

"You don't get it." Wulf glared at me. "If I don't show up with Vix by tomorrow, Pyxis will take my daughter on Tuesday. I'm not an idiot. Do you really think I can convince the cops to call the FBI, convince the FBI that I'm telling the truth, and then get a judge to sign a search warrant, all before Tuesday?"

Shit.

"They wouldn't need a search warrant if the owner said they could come onto the property," I pointed out. "Who owns the place?"

"Ted and Pauline Melbourne, Rita Groves, and Casey Canaveral bought the land decades ago," Wulf said. "Casey died last year and left it to Pyxis."

Damn.

"You're not a father, are you?" Wulf suddenly asked.

"I'm not," I admitted.

"That's why you don't get it. When Pyxis gave me the chance to save her, I had to take it," Wulf continued. "Andrea is only eleven. I can't...." He shook his head. "I know it makes me an awful person to plead for my sister to sacrifice herself, and there's no justifying it. But, I have to do it..."

"There has to be another way."

"There isn't," Vix interrupted. She stood up. "We're out of time, and I'm going back."

There was a moment of silence when the proverbial pin could've been heard dropping.

Then I exploded. "Like hell you are! I won't let you!"

The look she gave me was scorching and not in a good way. With a voice as cold as ice, she said, "It's not up to you. My brother is right. This is the only way we're guaranteed to save Andrea. I'm going."

Fuck.

THIRTY-FIVE
VIX

My gut feeling about Pyxis from our first meeting three years ago had been correct. He charmed his way in or out of most things, and the rest he would take by force.

However, the idea of him near my niece or the other young girls caused a terror that went to my very bones. I couldn't let that happen, no matter how I felt about going back.

I understood why Carson wouldn't let me go. But it was my decision to make, not his.

"You've heard what Wulf said about Pyxis not letting people leave," Carson said. "If you go up there by yourself, you might never get out again."

"I'm well aware of that," I said tightly as I struggled to push down the panic.

"Then stay." Carson turned the full force of those baby blue eyes on me. "Please, Vix."

I needed to go. Waiting would only add to my anxiety. Still, I owed him at least a few minutes.

"Come with me." I didn't want to discuss this in front of Wulf, so I took Carson into the guest bedroom and closed the door.

"Vix, don't do this. We can go to the police and convince them to get the FBI involved right away. Let the authorities handle it, Vix. It's insane to go yourself."

"Maybe they could eventually help," I admitted. "But even if you tell FBI Pyxis' plan for Tuesday, that doesn't mean they'll be able to cut through all the red tape to get there in time."

"I'm sure they have emergency guidelines," he argued.

"And what if they don't?" I asked. "What if they require physical proof before they can step foot on the commune? What if Wulf's word isn't good enough to get them to go in without a warrant? Pyxis could claim the commune is a religious institution and use it to keep the authorities away."

"That's a hell of a lot of 'what if's'," Carson said. "If you tell the FBI all of this, they'll know what to do to make sure nothing happens."

I was an optimistic person, but I didn't share his faith in the justice system.

"And what happens when Wulf shows up without me?" I asked quietly. "Pyxis might decide not to wait until Tuesday to take Andrea. He might make an example of this for the others."

"You don't know that he'll do anything," Carson

said. He crossed his arms, a stubborn look on his face. "Hell, for all you know, Wulf is lying. Did you think of that?"

"He's not."

"How do you know for sure?" Carson pushed, but the desperate note in Carson's words told me he saw the anguish and helplessness on Wulf's face, just as I did. The emotions were genuine.

"I don't have the time and luxury to come up with wild ideas and hope it doesn't put the people I love at risk. "

Carson paced the short length of the room. He finally stopped and looked at me. "If you would've told me about all this when Wulf first showed up, we would've had the time to get the police and FBI involved." He didn't yell, but there was no mistaking his primary emotion right now. "All of those kids could've been safe already."

"You must not have a very high opinion of me if you think I could've known for nearly a week and not done something about it." My hands curled into fists to keep them from shaking. "Because, of course, you're the one who would've figured it all out."

"That's not what I meant."

I shook my head. "It doesn't matter." I gestured between us. "We don't matter. Not as much as my niece and those other girls."

"There's nothing I can say to change your mind, is there?" His lips pressed into a flat line.

"No, there's not." I opened the door and stood to

the side. "I'll leave the key on the counter and the door unlocked."

"Vix."

"We're done here." The words tore at me, and I could barely breathe. I didn't know what would happen when I reached the commune, but I couldn't see a way to come out of this undamaged.

I saw my pain reflected in Carson's eyes, but only for a moment before he gave me a curt nod and walked out of the apartment.

I didn't follow him. He knew the way, and I had packing to do.

I filled my suitcase with the few items I'd purchased since coming here, leaving any of Carson's items. I cast one last glance at my room and headed into the living room where Wulf waited. He started toward the door, then paused. Without looking at me, he said, "Thank you."

I swallowed hard, unable to find an appropriate response to match the chaos I was feeling. He kept going, leaving me behind to put my key on the counter and turn off the last of the lights.

I doubted I'd see any of my things—or Carson—again.

With that sobering thought, I joined my brother in the garage. He was on the phone, ending the call as I stepped off the elevator.

"...tonight, right, Pyxis. We'll be there."

THIRTY-SIX
CARSON

I LEFT THE APARTMENT AND WENT TO MY STUDIO. How could I accept Vix sacrificing herself? She deserved to be safe and choose what she wanted for her life. To find happiness.

Those things were true, but my anger and hurt stemmed from something more selfish.

How could she choose that future over one with me?

Logically, I knew I couldn't expect her to put being with me higher than saving her niece, and I didn't expect it of her. But that didn't diminish the feeling I'd been abandoned. That she didn't choose to stay with me.

Dammit!

I wanted to hit something. Throw something. Cause the kind of destruction that would show my inner turmoil. I could feel the thread keeping me together, straining, and I didn't know what caused it to give after all these years.

I slammed my hands down on the counter and closed my eyes.

Long breaths.

My anger began to bleed away, but the hurt that replaced it was worse. Losing Vix to a normal break-up would've been awful, but knowing her fate brought me to my knees.

How could I move on with my life knowing Vix was a captive at the commune? Being hurt. Being raped. I shook my head.

I had to save her.

Even if she would hate me for it.

I needed to get to her before she left with Wulf.

I hurried back to the garage and up the stairs. I knocked on the door and reached for the doorknob, but before it turned, my heart sank. She was already gone. When I stepped inside the apartment, I saw the keys on the counter.

Dammit!

I needed to figure out how to rescue Vix without putting everyone else in danger. It couldn't be a one-time solution either. Pyxis had to be completely stopped.

A man like that wouldn't respond to reason and logic. He was hungry for power and a skillful manipulator. But without willing eyewitnesses from the commune, like Wulf and Vix, I wasn't sure of the best way to handle this.

A DRESS FOR CURVES

It wasn't until I glanced at the large flower arrangement sitting on my lounge table, a "thank you" gift from my sister Maggie for designing her wedding dress, that I realized I knew someone with a much better understanding of the law.

Stellan Brockmire.

He was a lawyer, and my new brother-in-law, Drake's uncle. I didn't know Stellan's legal specialty, but he'd know more than me.

I grabbed the key and locked the door behind me. I pulled out my phone and called Drake as I headed to the garage.

"Carson, how are you?"

"The jury's still out on that," I said. "I'll explain later. Not to be abrupt, but I'm in a time crunch. I need to talk to Stellan but don't have his number."

"Of course," Drake said. After giving the number, he asked, "Is everything all right?"

"It's a long story," I said as I got into my car. "I'll fill you and Maggie in when I can."

"Sure thing. If there's anything you need, just ask. We're family."

I thanked him and ended the call to place another.

"Hi, Stellan, it's Carson McCrae. Maggie's brother."

"Oh, hello." Stellan didn't hide his surprise.

"I have an issue that needs some legal advice and wondered if I could stop by and have a chat." I got right to the point.

"Sure, come by my office tomorrow."

"It's urgent, I'm afraid."

Stellan didn't hesitate. "No problem. Come to my place now," he said and gave me his address.

STELLAN GREETED me warmly after I knocked on his door, and I saw the curiosity in his eyes.

"I wouldn't have asked to come by your home like this unless it was urgent," I said.

"I assumed as much," Stellan said. "Now, is this a formal legal matter or advice between friends over a drink?"

My surprise must've shown on my face because he laughed.

"We rarely indulge during the day," Benjamin spoke up from a doorway. "But every so often, we make an exception. Would you care to join us, or is it more of an attorney-client-privilege sort of meeting?"

Some of the tension I'd been holding eased. "I could sure use a drink, and I would value your opinion too, Benjamin. A neutral third party might be just what I need."

"Shannon's?" Benjamin asked and held up the bottle.

"Please," I said. Now that the adrenaline was wearing off, I was afraid I'd crash. As I followed the couple into the living room, I knew I'd made the right call by coming here. They were close enough to me to make me feel comfortable but not so close that their emotions would cloud their judgment.

After downing the whisky, I laid everything out, from Vix leaving the commune to what Wulf told me about Pyxis, using Andrea as blackmail. The stormy expression on Benjamin's and Stellan's faces was confirmation enough. They would help me.

A few moments of silence passed as the pair processed all the information. Stellan was the first to speak.

"I'm not a criminal lawyer," he said. "But I know a couple of prosecutors who'll be eager to take down someone like that. And having a civil rights attorney in this situation seems like a pretty good idea, too."

"We've got the connections to make sure this gets to the right people," Benjamin said. "Now, first things first. Where, exactly, is this commune?"

Shit. I had no idea.

THIRTY-SEVEN
VIX

Wulf still wasn't much of a talker. He didn't say a word as he drove us out of the city, but I wasn't in a talkative mood anyway. I was more about trying not to cry at the moment.

We were in the car for nearly ninety minutes when I felt my phone vibrate with an incoming text. I didn't bother looking at it. It was probably Carson, and I didn't want to read yet another reason to why I was making a mistake.

Who knew if I'd ever see him again? I could pretend all I wanted, act as if I still saw the glass as half full, but I knew the truth. What I was doing was dangerous on too many levels to think I would get a happy ending.

First, though, I needed to find out what I was up against.

Since Wulf didn't offer any explanations, I took the initiative. "What happened?"

He glanced at me. "What happened when?"

"What happened back home? Pyxis was a jerk before, but people could always leave."

The surprise on Wulf's face was almost comical. "You happened."

I had a sinking feeling. "What do you mean?"

"When Pyxis found out you were gone, he went nuts," Wulf explained. "He found out that Roxie Dyson and the Tremaine family left, too."

"They went before me," I said. "It wasn't like they tried to hide it."

"But you did."

I nodded. "Of course. I'm not an idiot. Pyxis would try to stop me."

"Yeah," Wulf agreed. "He was so pissed he trashed his room and left."

That surprised me. "He left?"

Wulf nodded. "Yep. For four days, he was gone. Then he returned with his buddies. Then he called a meeting. While everyone was there, he introduced his buddies and all the guns–"

"What an asshole."

"He said they were for protecting the commune and then decided that you leaving was exactly the reason they needed protection," Wulf continued. "He told everyone you agreed to be his, but then the outside world seduced you. You left him and all of us. That you had betrayed us all. He said they couldn't risk you coming back and corrupting anyone, so we had to put up a fence and guards."

I felt sick. Pyxis used my escape to trap everyone else.

Wulf continued, "He said you intended to create chaos for the commune and convince the authorities to come and ruin the life we had. He made everyone afraid."

"Bastard," I breathed. "He's turned everybody against me."

Wulf glanced at me.

"Did you believe him?" I asked. "About me?"

"Maybe at first." Wulf's hands tightened on the wheel. "But then more stuff happened. I realized he was pressuring women to have sex with him, and I thought it was disgusting. I saw he was using you to put fear in people and get everything he wanted." Wulf glanced at me. "I'm sorry it took me so long to get to this point, Vix."

I nodded and thanked him, then went back to watching the scenery and wondering what would happen when we finally arrived at the commune.

By the time we turned onto the gravel road to the commune's driveway, the tension in the car had skyrocketed. My nerves were stretched thin, and Wulf gripped the steering wheel with white knuckles.

"We have to hand over our phones at the gate." He broke the silence.

"I figured as much," I said as I took my phone out of my pocket. I didn't look at it, not wanting to see how many messages I had from Carson.

That part of my life was over, and the sooner I accepted it, the better.

"You said 'our phones.' That means only Pyxis has access to a cell phone."

"Yeah, and his guards," Wulf said.

I caught sight of something between the trees that distracted me. A tall chain-link fence.

Damn.

"He added the barbed wire at the top a year ago when he caught a kid trying to climb over," Wulf said. "There's only one way in now, through the gate. He always has two people watching the gate, and no one gets in without prior approval."

Although the lighting was dim this time of day, I could see signs every few feet, alternating between 'No Trespassing' and 'Violators Will Be Shot.' The first ones had been there for years to show where our property line ended, but the second ones were new.

"The guards at the gate are armed," Wulf continued.

We turned into the driveway and immediately came to a gate across the width of the drive. There was a gatehouse with two people sitting in it.

"What's in it for them? His buddies, I mean. What do they get out of it?"

"What do you think?" He looked at me. "The commune looks up to them as protectors. Of course, they get all the free sex they desire and a share of the profits."

"What profits?" I was confused. The commune

was never about creating income. We only gathered what we consumed.

"That's right. That all started after you left." Wulf took a deep breath. "Pyxis is cultivating cannabis. Lots of it."

Holy shit. That explained everything. Except why Pyxis was so fixated on me. Maybe because I stood up to him and left?

"There are cameras everywhere now," Wulf said as he waved to the guys in the booth. "They have monitors out here and in the security office."

"There's a security office?"

"The library's now the security office and 'rehabilitation center'...basically, a couple of cells." He gave me a grim look. "I'm guessing that's where they'll put you, at least overnight, so security can monitor you."

The two men from the security booth were unknown to me. It must be two of Pyxis' buddies.

"Well, well, well, the warrior has returned home with his prey." The guy leered at me as Wulf rolled down the window. "Great job, Wulf."

"Here." Wulf held out our phones. "Where am I taking her?"

"You can hand her over to me." His gaze ran over me. "I'll take care of her."

"I don't think so," Wulf said, his voice sharp. "I'm not trusting her to anyone but Pyxis. I'm not risking fucking anything up."

"Pyxis's not back yet. Take her to the rehabilitation center," he said.

It was a relief I didn't have to face Pyxis right away. I could use the time to think. About what was to come. On how to save Andrea and the other girls. How to get rid of Pyxis and restore my childhood home.

It would prevent me from thinking about the life I could've had or the people I'd left behind—especially the man I could've loved.

If I didn't already.

THIRTY-EIGHT
CARSON

Proof.

Evidence.

Facts.

Shit.

I understood the legal system couldn't work on word of mouth alone. And most of the time, I agreed with that.

Except not right now.

Stellan took notes while I explained before asking questions, pointing out our problems.

Like the location of the commune.

I knew it was in upstate New York. That was about it.

Fuck.

"Does it have a name?" he asked. "Often places like that do."

I shook my head. "If it does, neither of them mentioned it."

"Do you know how far away it is?" Benjamin asked. "Maybe that will help us narrow it down."

I frowned. "She didn't say exactly, but it sounded like it was a few hours."

Benjamin and Stellan exchanged glances that couples had, which said a million things without a word.

"What is it?" I asked.

"Without a precise location, it'll be...difficult," Benjamin said carefully. "Especially if time is as short as you say."

"But not knowing should mean that we can get the FBI involved, right?"

"We can go to the FBI," Stellan said. "Kidnapping is their field, and child abuse and sexual assaults will certainly get their attention."

"Okay then, let's go." I stood up.

"Wait." Stellan motioned for me to sit down again.

"What's the problem?"

"The problem is they can't get a warrant on your word alone. I'm sure they'll look into it, but it'll take time."

"Time we don't have," I said.

"I know." He looked as frustrated as I. "Let me make some calls."

I texted Vix again to get more information, but still no response. I even reached out to the PI, who had helped me before, but he couldn't do anything without a location. A couple of hours later, I felt even worse, which I hadn't thought was possible.

We had nothing.

Stellan and Benjamin hit the same walls, even after a friend ran the name Pyxis Machoi through the criminal databases they had access to. Either the guy wasn't using his real name, or Pyxis didn't have any criminal history.

"We're not giving up," Stellan insisted as he watched me wear a path in his expensive carpet.

I stopped and gave him the closest thing to a smile I could manage. "You guys, I really appreciate this. I know it's not your usual thing, and it's the weekend."

"I've been fighting against injustice since I was fifteen," Stellan said. "I don't like to see anyone taken advantage of or hurt. Scumbags who mess with women and kids are the worst."

"Plus, you're family." Benjamin clapped a hand on my shoulder. "We take care of our own."

"Thank you." I meant the words, but I wish the circumstances had been different.

"I have a couple of people looking into some things for me, but I've exhausted my list until we have more information."

I pulled my phone from my pocket and checked it. Again.

"I texted Vix for an address, but still nothing," I said, trying not to let my voice show how much her lack of contact bothered me.

"She might not have her phone?" Benjamin said.

"It wasn't in the apartment," I said, frowning. "But I didn't exactly search the place."

"Do you think she might've left something behind that could give us the location of the commune?"

Stellan's question made me want to kick myself. I'd been right there and never thought to look for anything like that.

"Since we're stuck with other options, go check it out. And if there's nothing, get something to eat, try to grab a couple of hours of sleep," Benjamin said.

"Sleep?"

Benjamin's smile was sympathetic. "I know you want to be doing things, but until we have something new, we're in a holding pattern. You need to take care of yourself if you're going to be any good to her."

He was right, no matter how much I didn't like it. "All right. I'll call you if I find anything."

"And I'll call as soon as we hear anything from our end," Stellan promised.

Leaving without a plan frustrated me, but I didn't see any options. We could only hope to find a clue. I headed out and drove back to my studio, as I kept hoping for a call or a text with more information. Nothing came.

After I went inside the apartment, I searched around the kitchen first. Then I moved to the living room, the guest room, and the bathroom. Nothing.

Finally, I went to her bedroom. She'd left a few things on the bedside table and dresser—every picture and item. I knew the story behind some, but even those didn't reveal anything relevant to the current situation.

I turned my attention to her dresser drawers, hoping she hid something.

And again, nothing.

No phone.

It wasn't here.

"Fuck." I rubbed my forehead as I spotted her laptop. I needed a drink before looking into that.

I kept a bottle of my brother Brody's best whisky in my studio, and I trudged back upstairs with it. I didn't bother with a glass as I settled on the couch and turned on the laptop.

While I waited for it to boot, I opened the whisky and took a fortifying swig before a password box showed up.

"Dammit." I took another drink.

Maybe I could guess her password. I tried everything I knew about her. Names, dates, favorite things. It didn't work. I didn't know her as well as I thought. I threw the laptop on her bed.

I failed her, just like I failed Maggie.

I didn't remember falling asleep, or passing out. The last thing I remembered was the whisky bottle and thinking I needed water. Then, I woke up to a pounding headache and a mouth that felt like I'd been sucking on shit-flavored cotton balls.

But I had an idea.

As I staggered to the bathroom, I pulled up a phone number. I had a favor to ask.

THIRTY-NINE
VIX
THREE YEARS AGO.

I didn't like him. The new guy.

With his smug, smarmy smile and his expensive clothes.

"Hey, Vixen." Wulf smiled at me. "I'd like you to meet Pyxis Machoi. Pyxis, this is my little sister, Vixen Teal."

"Vixen." He seemed to savor the sound of my name as he held out his hand.

I knew that, in polite society, refusing to shake someone's hand was frowned on, even if people didn't like touching strangers. Fortunately, one of the best things about living here was that we didn't need to conform to societal standards if we didn't want to.

And I most definitely didn't want to.

"Welcome," I said, giving him a smile but not my hand.

Something cold flickered in his eyes, but the smile

never left his lips. "I don't remember you from when I was here as a teenager."

"She was six," Wulf said.

"That explains it." His gaze ran down my body and up again, the lazy perusal that told me he was accustomed to his attention being welcomed. "You've grown up nicely."

"Wulf," I ignored Pyxis's compliment. "I'm going to take Andrea to the garden. Is she here?"

"She is." Wulf looked relieved. "Thank you. Pyxis asked if I could show him around."

"You two know each other?" I didn't bother to hide my surprise.

"We hung out when he was here as a teenager," Wulf explained. "When he came back, he remembered me."

Now I understood why my brother was so willing to cancel plans with his daughter. Wulf didn't have many friends. Not because he was disliked, exactly, but he'd always been, well, needy. Someone like Pyxis remembering him would be a big deal for Wulf.

"You go ahead then," I said. "I'll let Andrea know that you're giving a tour."

As Wulf and Pyxis walked away, I could feel the latter's eyes on me, and I hoped the other commune members would get the same unsettled feeling about the newcomer as I did and vote not to allow him to join. Something about him made me think his presence would bring changes, and not in a good way.

When my niece called my name, I pushed away

those thoughts and found a genuine smile curving my lips. While I felt my concerns were valid, I wouldn't dwell on them now. I had an excited eight-year-old to spend time with, and I refused to give her anything less than my complete and undivided attention. Besides, nothing was being decided right now. I'd have plenty of time to find out what everyone else thought and convince them if necessary. Everything would be fine.

I refused to believe otherwise.

FORTY VIX

PRESENT DAY

Disoriented, I struggled to remember where I was, and why nothing felt familiar. The bed was uncomfortable, a far cry from the quality mattress I had at Carson's apartment. The air had a chemical smell that took me a moment to place as disinfectant or cleaning product. Then I heard footsteps, shoes on some sort of hard surface, and things came flooding back on a wave of adrenaline.

Shit.

I was back, and *not* voluntarily.

Well, sort of. Technically, I agreed to come back, but it was under duress, and I wouldn't count that.

I blinked against the darkness, my mind racing. Instincts warred between fight and flight, but I knew neither one would be a viable option at the moment. I needed to stay calm, no matter who came through the door. I still couldn't see.

An overhead light came on, and I was momentarily

blinded. I didn't, however, need to see to recognize the voice.

"Hey, Vix. Didn't think I'd see you again."

Zhora Grey was twenty-two the last time I saw her, and she hadn't changed a bit. It'd only been two years, but she should've changed at least a little. Instead, even her chin-length black hair was the same. But when I met her gaze, I saw a change. Her hazel eyes, always so bright and sweet, were shadowed and haunted.

"Welcome back."

Zhora's smile might've looked normal to anyone else, but I'd known her my whole life. Zhora and I were like sisters.

"I'm not really sure how welcomed I feel." I gestured around the room.

"Yeah, things have changed," Zhora said. "You still look good, though."

I didn't know if she would want a hug, but something told me she needed one. I opened my arms, and relief crossed her face before she fell into my embrace. There, for a moment, I was glad I'd come back. Andrea and my parents weren't the only ones I'd missed.

Then Zhora pulled back, and the moment was broken.

"I'm supposed to take you to him." She didn't look happy about it.

I wouldn't make things harder for her. "All right. Let's go."

"I already signed you out," she said as we left what had once been our library.

Stepping outside, I breathed in the crisp morning air. I loved my life in the city, but nothing there smelled like this. We were officially a day away from autumn, but it already felt like my favorite time of year, when the leaves started to turn, and nature exploded into all of its beauty.

"I heard you've been living in the city," Zhora said as she led me toward the largest of the houses. "Did you like it there? I'd think it'd be...overcrowded."

"It definitely takes some getting used to," I admitted. "And there were things I missed here."

"Not enough to come back on your own," she said.

I heard no judgment in her voice, but I suspected she felt more than she let on.

We stopped in front of a house, and Zhora knocked on the door before stepping back.

I didn't recognize the man who answered, but Zhora did. She glared at him, and he returned the look, making me think they weren't fond of each other.

"I brought Vix like Pyxis asked," she said.

"Come in," the guy said, stepping to the side.

"Just her," Zhora said. "I'm going to breakfast."

The guy shrugged and looked at me. "Let's go."

When I passed him to enter the house, I saw a handgun tucked in the waistband of his jeans.

The last time I was in this house, I'd dropped off food for Wulf because he was sick. It used to look like all the other homes, but now, the front room housed a vast amount of electronics. A big screen TV, gaming systems, laptops, things that in the past were shared in the main hall, if the commune had them at all. I suspected only Pyxis lived here, rotating guards in and out. And probably the same for women too.

My stomach clenched as I followed the blond guy up the stairs. Pyxis wanted a big ceremony tomorrow, but that didn't mean he would wait for sex. I needed to be prepared. For the sake of everybody, I might have to give in.

The guy stopped in front of the first door and knocked. "She's here."

A voice called out, "Send her in."

He opened the door and gestured for me to enter. I stepped into a small office where the walls were covered with pictures and diplomas. A bookshelf with leather-bound volumes was to the right. A large wooden desk sat on the far side of the room, and behind it, a man who looked the same as he did when I left two years ago.

The leer he gave me was the same too.

"You look good, Vixen." He motioned to the chair on my side of the desk. "Have a seat."

I didn't want to do *anything* he asked, but it was better to choose my battles.

I took a seat.

"How are you?"

I folded my hands in my lap. "Not great, actually. I came here voluntarily after you sent Wulf to get me, then as soon as I arrived, I'm locked up in a tiny room with an uncomfortable bed." I took pride in my ability to keep my voice even.

"I'm sorry it had to be like that," he said smoothly. "I just couldn't be sure it was safe."

"You thought I'd be in danger?" That was a joke.

"You left rather suddenly, without talking to anyone. Some people might've taken that badly." He smirked. "But no, your safety wasn't my primary concern."

My eyes widened. "You think *I'm* dangerous?"

"I don't know, Vixen." His voice sounded sincere. "You've been gone for two years in a dangerous world. How can I know you haven't...changed?"

I kept my tone as innocent as possible. "If you're worried about me putting your people at risk, I'm happy to go back to New York."

Something dark flickered across his eyes. "Back to selling yourself to the highest bidder?"

I clenched my teeth for a moment before speaking. "I think you've misunderstood what I've been doing in New York. I work in retail."

He raised an eyebrow. "Retail? I've been to a few cities, and I can't think of a single retail job that includes prancing around half-dressed for a group of men and the entire internet."

"I modeled for a world-renowned designer." I refused to let him shame me. "A one-time thing. I worked at a boutique for nearly two years and just started working at a new one."

"A one-time thing," Pyxis said. "Because you know you shouldn't be showing your body to strangers."

He made it a statement, but I knew he wanted an answer.

"No, because it was a fun thing to try once, but not something I would want to pursue a career in." I folded my arms. "I plan on sticking with sales."

He smiled widely. "Well, now, see, I have great news about that. You don't need to work anymore. You're home."

"This isn't my home anymore," I said, keeping my voice firm but not aggressive. "I have a home and a life in New York."

His smile faded. "*This* is your home."

An uncomfortable silence fell between us.

"I think you need to be reminded of that," he said suddenly. "You'll spend today in the rehabilitation center and go over the new required reading. I'll have my men bring you your meals."

I didn't like the sound of being locked up again, but at least I avoided his touch today. I'd take a day of reprieve.

"Tomorrow, you'll spend time with your family and get to know your home again."

I wanted to kick him in his balls.

"Tuesday is, of course, the Autumnal Equinox," he continued. "If you recall that from your time here. We will have a ceremony where we'll be joined." His gaze dropped to my chest, slid down, and then back up. "After which, we'll immediately consummate our relationship and then return to the celebration so that everyone can see that you're mine."

"And if I say 'thanks, but no thanks?'" I asked.

His eyes narrowed, all traces of that charm and humor gone. "That would be...unwise."

"Think about it, Pyxis," I said. "Wouldn't it be better to have people who want to be with you?"

He leaned forward and put his arms on the desk. "*I* decide what happens here. *I* choose who and what I want. This place and everyone here is *mine*." He paused and then said, "And you're going to clarify that you're doing this of your own free will."

"I am?"

He scowled at me. "You are, or there will be consequences. Namely, your niece, Andrea, will become my counterpart for the ceremony."

My stomach twisted, and I curled my hands into fists to stop myself from doing something rash. I refused, however, to curb my tongue. "You promised Wulf you'd leave Andrea alone if I came back."

"What part of 'everyone here is mine' don't you understand?" Pyxis asked. "It's simple. Either you or Andrea will be claimed at the Autumn Equinox ceremony. If I can't have you, I'll take the virgin."

As fury roiled inside me, I barely registered the pain of my nails cutting into my palms. Any hope of reasoning with Pyxis was gone.

FORTY-ONE
CARSON

I'd finally called my brother, Eoin. I don't know why I hadn't thought of him before now. Eoin was ex-Army and spent most of his time deployed overseas until recently. After he nearly died in an ambush, he transitioned into civilian life, and now he was a part of a private security team.

Eoin didn't hesitate despite his newborn baby when I explained the situation this morning. He told me his team would fly in this evening on a private plane.

After reaching the airport in a rented van, I pulled into the parking area for private planes, and I watched as the men stepped off the plane.

Jesus. What just rolled into town?

Not a single guy under six feet, all looking like they could break a person in half without even trying.

"Thanks for coming," I said as I gave Eoin a quick hug.

"Of course." He looked tired but happy. Being a father suited him, and I did not doubt being a husband would, too. He and Aline were set to marry the weekend before Thanksgiving.

"Carson, it's nice to put a face with a name." A man with short blond hair and dark eyes held out a hand. "I'm Cain Hudson."

I recognized the name. He was the group leader, a former intelligence officer who knew Eoin from their days in the Army. He was probably only a few years older than me. I shook his hand.

"I appreciate you guys coming on such short notice," I said.

"Family comes first," Cain said. He pointed to a lean young man with white-blond hair. "That's Bode, but we call him Bruce."

"As in Wayne," Bruce said with an easy grin that lit up his green eyes. "Good to meet you."

"I'm Dez." With dark brown hair and a scar through his eyebrow, the man strapped down a massive duffel bag.

"That one's Pollard, but everyone calls him Fever." Eoin gestured to the only man left. He was broad and had the stern look of someone not to mess with.

"Everything packed up?" Cain asked.

"We're good to go," Dez answered.

Eoin sat in the passenger seat as his buddies climbed into the back with the ease of men who were trained for this. Once they were all settled, I pulled away from the parking area.

"I'll thoroughly analyze this Machoi character," Cain said. "Fever will pull up maps and satellite images to see what they can tell us."

"Great," I said.

"Dez and Bruce will need every detail you have heard about the commune. Anything that can translate into a physical detail," Cain continued.

"Like what?"

"Do they live in houses? What size? That sort of thing," Bruce said.

"And that'll help you find it?"

"We're looking for more than her location. We need to know as much as possible about what we're up against."

"And we can get to her that much faster," Eoin explained. "Going in blind is dangerous for everyone."

"Well, that's the problem," I said. "Vix talked very little about her life before coming to the city."

"You might know more than you realize," Cain said. "Anything's better than nothing."

I should know more, but besides her sexual preferences, I hardly knew her. Everything was still so new.

As I made my way to my place, I let my mind drift into that slightly fuzzy place where driving was automatic, and the conversation was background noise.

We didn't venture into more heavy stuff until we were in my apartment, their bags piled in one corner of my living room and a stack of pizza boxes on the dining room table. After eating in silence for a couple of minutes, Cain opened a notebook and looked at me.

"All right, what do you know about Pyxis Machoi?"

"Not a lot," I said. "Um, he didn't grow up in the commune. He's only been there for a few years. Three, I think. He was there for a bit before Vix left, and that was two years ago."

"That's good," he said, jotting down notes. "Anything else?"

"He inherited the property when the last of the original owners died."

"Do you remember their names?" Cain asked.

I gave him the names and information as best as I could remember, but it didn't seem like much. The others had notebooks and asked questions that prompted memories of things Vix and Wulf had said.

"Do you think this will help?" I wanted to hope, but it seemed like a long shot.

"I never promise that we'll succeed," Cain said. "But we're all damn good at our jobs, so I have no problem promising we'll do everything possible." He set down his pen. "If we find her, we'll get her back."

I appreciated the honesty, though I wished Cain could've given me more hope.

"What do I do now?" I asked.

"Have you spoken to any of her friends since she left?" Eoin asked.

"No. Besides you, the only people I talked to were Stellan Brockmire and Benjamin Mac Gilleain, my brother-in-law's uncle. Stellan is a lawyer."

"Go on," Dez said.

"Stellan said we didn't have enough for a search warrant." I didn't hide the disappointment in my voice.

"That's why we exist," Cain said. "To do things the cops can't. Of course, nothing illegal, usually, but we can...bend rules that cops can't."

"It's not about bringing people to justice," Eoin added. "We have specific goals in mind. Here, the objective is to rescue Vix. We're not arresting Pyxis and putting him on trial.

"Why don't you reach out to Vix's friends," Cain said. "Find out if any of them have information about Pyxis and the commune."

"I'll do that." I stood and gathered the paper plates.

"Let's get to work," Cain said.

I threw away the trash and took my phone into one of the guest rooms to avoid disturbing the others.

My models were my first calls. I kept it simple, but unfortunately, they knew even less than I did about that part of Vix's life.

I could only think of three other people, though I doubted any of the Devereauxes would talk to me.

The last was Vix's roommate, Susanna.

It took me a while, but eventually, I tracked down her number. My call went to voice mail, and I left a message, asking her to call me back because Vix was in trouble. I hoped that would be enough.

It took less than half an hour before my phone rang. I recognized the number, and a wave of relief washed over me.

"Carson?" Susanna sounded concerned. "What's wrong with Vix?"

"She's left, possibly in danger, and I'm trying to find her. What do you know about where she grew up?" I asked.

"Not a lot," she said, the concern now tempered with confusion. "I got the impression she didn't have a traditional family, and I know she didn't live in the city. But I do not know where exactly."

I sighed, my last hope dashed. "Dammit. I was hoping you might have a clue that could help me find her."

"What happened?"

"Her brother showed up here and forced her to go back. I can't go into much detail."

"That's okay...oh, I just remembered something!" Susanna blurted out. "She said the commune was near a small town. Big enough to have a tourist industry for nature stuff like hiking trails. I know it's not much."

"No, Susanna, it's more than I had before," I said honestly. "Thank you."

"I'll try to call her and let you know if I hear from her," she said.

After I ended the call, I told the new information to Eoin.

"It's not much," Eoin said with a frustrated sigh. "Your girl hardly has any footprint online. No social media at all. What twenty-something person doesn't have any social media? How did her brother find her?" Eoin asked.

"That is my fault," I admitted. "Vix modeled for me in a fashion show, and we streamed it online."

"That seems kind of random," Eoin said with a frown. "He just found that stream?"

"I don't know how he found it."

"I do," Cain spoke up from the other side of the room. "At least, I have a theory."

I raised a brow in curiosity.

"Pyxis Machoi doesn't exist."

That got everyone's attention.

"I looked into legal name changes. That's where I found the name Conwell Plue Dickie, Jr."

"That's one hell of a name," Eoin said. "I can see why he wanted to change it. Though Pyxis Machoi wouldn't have been my first choice."

"He made the change about four years ago," Cain continued. "Then, searching his birth name, I found something. He grew up in a small town. He graduated from NYU double majored in psychology and social work, and worked in the computer department."

"That means he's tech-savvy," I said.

"It looks like he tried to erase any connection between his new name and the old one. I also ran a check for a criminal record and found none. The guy is clean."

"If he didn't have a criminal history, aside from having a pretty shitty name, why'd he change it?" I asked.

"Maybe he just wanted a cool name. It's hard to

convince people you're special if your name is Conwell Plue Dickie," Cain said with a laugh.

"We're going to find her." Eoin clapped his hand on my shoulder.

I really hoped so.

FORTY-TWO
VIX

Pyxis gave me reading materials. One was a print-out from a website titled "How Feminism Ruined Good Men." I read it, partly because I was bored but mostly because I needed to understand what Pyxis was filling everyone's heads with. I also had a book titled *How to Prepare for the Fall of Everything*. The internet manifesto's content was the same and equally disturbing. And a well-worn hardcover called *Submission: The Natural State*, which basically said most people didn't want freedom. They wanted to be told what to do and follow a vigorous leader. The author said people would be happier when they accepted this.

I was still mulling it over when I fell asleep, leading to some strange and disturbing dreams.

My head was cloudy when I woke up, and it took me a moment to remember where I was. It wasn't many days ago that I would wake up in a comfortable bed next to Carson, kiss him, and make love to him. I imagined waking up like that again and finding out that all of this was a bad dream.

Still, I didn't regret my decision to come back. I had my reasons.

The knock on the door startled me.

"Wake up, Vixen," Wulf called. "I'm supposed to take you to shower and change before you see your family."

As Wulf escorted me to the communal shower, I used the time to survey everything I missed yesterday. It felt different from when I was growing up. Some people smiled and laughed, but it didn't feel as easy or joyful as I remembered.

I took a quick and refreshing shower, then dressed in the strange clothes Wulf had brought. They took my suitcase from me, so I had no option but to pull on the shapeless gray dress.

"The ceremony tomorrow will be outside, but after, we'll be having a special meal in the main hall," Wulf said as I came out. "Pyxis assigned our family to decorate today so we can be productive while meeting together."

The first thing I noticed when we stepped into the main hall was that all the artwork was missing. The walls were blank, save for a single portrait at the far end, above the stage. One guess as to whose picture *that* was.

Then I saw my family.

My father, Oberlain, looked like he'd lost weight. His sandy brown hair was thinner, and he had new lines on his face. My mother was helping him hang a banner, looking the same until she turned to me, and I saw the shadows in her eyes.

"Vix!" Andrea ran from Anise's side, ignoring my sister's command to slow down.

My niece had changed the most while I was gone. Still slender, her face had lost its childishness. Her reddish-brown hair hung loosely past her shoulders instead of in the braids she favored not too long ago. The lack of fear in her cerulean blue eyes told me she didn't know why I was here or what fate I saved her from.

"Hey, sweetheart." I opened my arms to catch her as she hurled herself at me. "I've missed you."

"If you missed her so much, maybe you shouldn't have left." Anise's dark eyes were hard as she came over to me. "But I suppose you weren't thinking of anyone but yourself. As usual."

I ignored her and focused on Andrea. "Your dad told me you were doing really well in school."

"I am," she said proudly. "Phina says I'm like you in that way."

"Of course she does," Anise said loudly. "Perfect Vixen can do no wrong."

"Anise." Wulf's voice held a warning.

"Oh, sorry, Wulf. Am I not allowed to have an opinion now?" Anise said snidely. "I guess you're back in Pyxis's good graces, now."

"Andrea, honey, don't you need to be going?"

Phina said, her smile looking strained. "It's time to learn about the Autumn Equinox."

Andrea looked torn.

"Go ahead," I said, giving her another hug. "I'll see you later."

"You won't leave without saying goodbye?" she asked. "Not this time?"

My heart squeezed. "No, I won't leave without saying goodbye this time."

A wide smile broke across her face.

As she walked away, I knew that coming back had been the right thing to do, no matter what would happen to me.

"It's good to see you, Vix." Phina came over to embrace me, and I leaned into the contact. Our relationship might not have been a traditional mother and daughter, but I never doubted that she loved me.

I was counting on it for what came next.

"You know what Pyxis has planned for tomorrow, right?" I asked as I pulled back.

Phina's gaze slid away from me, and she shuffled uncomfortably. But Anise answered my question.

"Of course, we know. Everyone knows." She crossed her arms and glared at me. "You're being welcomed back with open arms and given the position any of us would kill to have."

For several seconds, I couldn't even speak. When I finally found my voice again, I directed everything at Anise. "Do you think I don't want any of this? Pyxis is the reason I left. I only came back because Wulf told me what Pyxis would do to the girls here."

"You couldn't even come back to visit?" Anise asked.

"And risk that mad man coming after me? No." I shook my head. "I refuse to apologize for protecting myself."

"Protecting yourself from what?" She threw up her hands. "From being claimed by Pyxis?"

"I don't want him."

"Is he not good enough for you?" Anise sniped. "Not enough money or prestige?"

"When have I ever cared about that?" I made it an honest question.

"Vix, can't you at least try to get along with Pyxis?" Phina asked. "If he's pleased, he'll treat you well."

"Won't it be nice to be home again?" Oberlain asked. "And you being with Pyxis will be good for all of us."

I looked at Wulf. "Do they know?"

He shook his head. "I didn't tell anyone."

"Tell anyone what?" Oberlain asked.

"Pyxis intended to claim Andrea tomorrow if I didn't come back," I said bluntly.

"No." Phina shook her head. "She's only eleven. No."

"She started her period," Wulf said, looking down at his feet. "You heard what Pyxis said about when girls 'became women.'"

"He didn't mean anyone *that* young," Oberlain said. "He couldn't. I mean, eleven?"

"He told me he would claim my daughter if I didn't get Vix to return." Wulf raised his head.

Anise shook her head. "He was just using some leverage to get you to do something you should've done for him without question. Pyxis wouldn't force anyone to do anything. Everything's consensual."

I raised an eyebrow. "You think an *adult* should be allowed to have sex with an eleven-year-old if that child says it's okay?"

"Pyxis wasn't being serious about that," she insisted. "Besides, just because he's claiming them in a ceremony doesn't mean he will have sex with them right away. And why would he want little girls when he can have any *woman* he wants?"

"Do you hear yourself?" I asked her. Then I looked at my parents. "Do any of you hear yourselves?"

Anise glared at me, but neither of my parents could meet my eyes.

"You sat back and did nothing when that man took over our home. You sat and did nothing when he announced all the women here belonged to him." I kept my voice even and low, but I didn't mask the disappointment and anger in my words. "When he locked everyone in and refused to let you leave, you did nothing."

"Vix–" Phina began.

I cut her off. "When Pyxis said that he would 'claim' *children*, none of you did anything. Now, Wulf is telling you this man intended to *rape* a member of our family—a child, no less—and the only way to stop him was if I took her place. You never stepped up to protect the people in this community the way you should have."

"That's not fair," Anise said. "You've been gone–"

"Yes, I left," I interrupted. "I left to protect myself. But as soon as I found out about this, I came back. I'm willing to sacrifice myself to protect Andrea and those other girls. And Wulf will do anything to protect his daughter. You three? You three won't risk anyone looking at you cross-eyed, even to protect innocents." I shook my head. "I'm ashamed to call you my family."

Without waiting for a response or for Wulf to escort me, I turned and walked out of the main hall back to my cell.

FORTY-THREE
CARSON

I WAS IN THE MIDDLE OF STARTING THE FIFTH POT of coffee for the day when Dez called out, "I think I found it."

I rushed into the living room, where the rest of the team was gathered.

"Those names you gave me," Dez said to me. "Of the original owners, I found them."

"How?" Cain asked.

"A deed of sale from a corporation to a group of four people: Ted and Pauline Melbourne, Rita Groves, and Casey Canaveral. A good chunk of land in upstate New York."

"Was it sold to Pyxis? Or Conwell Dickie?" I asked.

Dez shook his head. "There's no record of it. Pyxis being the landowner is a lie."

"I'm pretty confident this is the place," Cain said as

he peered over Dez's shoulder. "It also fits with what the roommate said about the place."

"I agree," Eoin said.

The other men echoed their agreement, and Dez pulled up a picture of the area. We couldn't see details, but we made out enough to see several buildings grouped together and what looked like a fence around the property.

"Can we get anything closer?" Cain asked. "I'd like to know what kind of fence that is and if there are any other fortifications in place."

Dez looked up at Cain. "Not with this software."

A look passed between the two of them.

"Give me a few minutes," Dez said.

Cain nodded. "Print up whatever you find." He turned to Fever. "We need a topographical map of the surrounding area and a larger copy of the layout of the commune."

Fever nodded and left.

"Carson, get the van gassed up and ready." Cain glanced at Eoin, who nodded once, as if in answer to something, "You'll need cash. A lot."

"You think Pyxis wants a payoff?"

"He's a greedy asshole. He might part with one… valuable asset for another," Cain said. "Plus, we don't want to leave a paper trail."

"Understood." I looked at my watch and frowned. "It's getting late. I need to go."

"Copy that," Eoin said. "We'll have a plan put together by the time you get back."

I grabbed the keys to the rental, my mind racing to determine how much cash I could get my hands on.

As I topped off the gas tank, I made a call to my bank, then placed a few other calls, each one reminding me I wasn't in this alone. I had family and friends behind me.

Forty minutes later, I left the bank with more money than I was comfortable carrying. With half a million dollars split between two briefcases, I felt like I had a target on my back.

I trusted the parking garage at my building, but I still tucked the briefcases under the seats and out of sight before locking the van and returning to my apartment.

As soon as I walked in, I felt the change in the atmosphere. The room practically buzzed with tension, and the men had their game faces on.

"Mission accomplished?" Cain asked.

I nodded. "We're all set."

"Okay, here's the plan," Eoin said. "We're leaving now and getting rooms in the town near the commune. First thing tomorrow morning, you and I will request a meeting with Pyxis. We'll try to reason with him. If that doesn't work, you offer him money."

"And if he doesn't agree to it?" I asked. "Or what if he'll only take money for Vix and not let the other girls go? Vix won't go if the others stay."

"Don't worry," Eoin assured me. "The plan is to take everyone who wants to go."

"And if he won't take the deal?"

"Things will then get a little more...complicated," Eoin said. "But we have a plan for that, too."

Finally, I could exhale. "Thank you," I said. "Seriously, thank you all for doing this."

"We're glad to help," Eoin said. "Now, let's get the last of our stuff together and go rescue a damsel in distress."

"Better not let her hear you call her than," I said. "She doesn't 'damsel.'"

"Noted," Eoin said. "Let's go get your girl, then."

FORTY-FOUR
CARSON

I wasn't sure what I'd expected from spending several hours in a van with five former military guys, but I quickly learned humor was how they kept their heads clear for the job.

We reached our destination, a small but quaint vacation town. The B&B was easy to spot, and we headed straight for it.

Since we didn't know the time for the ceremony, we got up at daybreak and were ready to go within minutes. We'd memorized every inch of both plans and were prepared, but I wasn't naïve enough to think that meant things would go smoothly, especially with a wild card like Pyxis. The others oozed confidence, and I used it to steel myself for what was about to go down.

We stopped about a mile from our destination, and everyone but Eoin and I got out. They scattered, disappearing into the trees on both sides of the road. While we were busy with Pyxis, they'd be getting the lay of the land, confirming things we knew, and making necessary changes.

The tree line ended a couple of yards later, revealing a tall fence with warning signs and barbed wire. Eoin let out a low whistle, and I cursed.

"Think that's for keeping people out or in?" he asked.

"Both," I said. "Pyxis doesn't want to risk a hiker stumbling onto the commune, realizing what's going on."

Spotting the gatehouse, we fell silent, focusing on what came next. Eoin turned off the gravel road and stopped in front of the gate. Inside the tiny building, I saw two men, one who looked to be in his mid-forties and heavy-set, the other younger and skinnier, maybe around Vix's age. Both carried semi-automatic rifles, and as they came out, I could see handguns.

Shit.

Nobody had mentioned weapons. How had Wulf missed mentioning this?

"It changes nothing," Eoin said quietly. "We're still going to get her out. Get all of them out."

I nodded.

Showtime.

"Good morning," I said.

"Turn around," the heavy-set guy said with no preamble. "This is private property."

"I know," I said evenly. "I'm here to speak with the owner. Pyxis Machoi."

The guy's eyes widened with surprise. "What?"

"Pyxis Machoi," I repeated. "I want to speak to him."

"Well...you can't." The heavy-set guy scowled. "Now go away."

"Shouldn't we call?" The skinny guy had left his position at Eoin's door and now stood over by his partner. "I mean, he knows–"

"He knows jack-shit," the larger guy snapped. "You know the rules."

"I think this gentleman here has the right idea," I said. "Call your boss and tell him he has two people who want to talk some business with him."

The big guy came close enough for me to smell bad breath. "If you know what's good for you, you'll turn around and go back wherever you came from."

I'd met his type before—a bully. I dealt with my fair share, and I'd handle him the same way. "I'm not going anywhere until I speak with Pyxis Machoi."

He stepped back, his hands tightening on the gun. I felt Eoin tense next to me, and my mind automatically went to the guns under our seats. Several tense seconds passed, and then a noise caught our attention. The gate slid open in front of us.

"What the fuck are you doin', Damon?"

"Pyxis said to let them through," the little guy called.

The guard moved away from the van. "Turn into the first parking lot and stay there until someone comes to take you to Pyxis. Don't go wandering around."

"Wouldn't dream of it," I said with a false smile.

As I pulled through the gate and drove up the driveway, Eoin said with a big smile, "Wouldn't dream of it?"

I glanced over to see him grinning at me. "Fuck you."

Another armed man already stood in the small parking lot, only big enough for about five cars. I pulled up next to the man and looked at Eoin.

"Let's go meet this son of a bitch," Eoin said.

"This way." The guy didn't introduce himself, he merely turned and started walking.

The three of us made our way across the parking lot. I kept my eyes on the guy, resisting the urge to see if I could spot Vix. Behind me, Eoin followed the plan and surveyed the area, noting everything. If he saw Vix, he'd tell me.

We stopped at a house more prominent than the others. We went up a set of stairs, and the guy knocked on the door.

"Come in."

The door opened, and I saw the man who'd scared Vix so badly that she left her family and life to get away from him. As I entered the room, my first impression was that he took advantage of the arrogance bleeding from his persona. He knew he was good-looking and used it to get his way. Or better, to manipulate people. And when his other tricks failed, he used intimidation.

"Hello." He smiled at us and stood, holding out a

hand like we were welcomed guests. "I'm Pyxis. I hear you wanted to do business."

"I'm Carson McCrae, and this is Eoin." I shook Pyxis's hand, ignoring how he tried to squeeze tighter than necessary. I found a bit of pleasure in how he winced when Eoin applied the same trick.

"Well, spill it, bro. What can I do you for?" he asked while rubbing his hand.

"You can start by opening your gate and letting everybody leave if they want to...bro."

He didn't bat an eye. "I assure you, Carson, that my people are always free to come and go as they please."

Eoin chuckled.

"Here's what I know," I said, looking Pyxis straight in the eyes. "I know you're threatening and intimidating every woman here into your bed." I fought to keep my voice even. "And I know that for you, 'women' means any female who's old enough to start her period."

Pyxis broke out in laughter. "I don't know who told you those gross and disturbing lies," Pyxis said, "but that's all they are. Lies. Everyone here is free to make whatever decisions they wish. I don't force anyone to do anything they don't want, and I certainly wouldn't harm children."

"All right, then you wouldn't mind us talking to your people. Find out what they think."

He shook his head, a condescending smile on his face.

"You see, I can't let you do that. It would be irresponsible of me to expose my people to outside influences. People here have no experience with the outside world. Merely speaking with you could corrupt their poor souls."

Enough with beating around the bush. "I want to talk to Vixen Teal," I said. "She knows me. Surely, a simple discussion with me won't cause her any harm."

His expression hardened. "No."

My eyebrows went up. This guy seemed like he enjoyed hearing himself talk but was not very helpful.

"I know who you are, Carson McCrae." Gone was the charming voice. "Vixen has no interest in seeing you. Don't you get it? She rejected you and came back to be with me. Like the gentleman I'm sure you are, you must respect her decision."

I was getting nowhere. It was time to step up my game. "Perhaps we can make some sort of arrangement," I said. "A place like this must be expensive to keep up. I have money. Money that I could…invest in your commune. In exchange for some of your…assets."

Saying the words, even as deception, made me sick to my stomach, but I didn't let it show on my face. For this to work, he had to believe I would buy women.

"My assets?" he echoed and started laughing, but I noticed the greed gleaming in his eyes.

"Vixen Teal and her niece, Andrea, to start," I said. "Maybe a few other girls of a certain age. I've got half a million in cash I can give you right now if you give me them."

He stared at me for a minute and then shook his

head, wariness surpassing his lust for money. "I'm insulted that you think I'm the kind of man who'd sell another human being. I think it's time for you two to go," he announced. "My men will escort you back to your vehicle. If I were you, I wouldn't come back. We shoot trespassers."Another dead-end. Fuck. Time for Plan B. "I'm sorry to hear, but if you change your mind, I'll be at the bed-and-breakfast," I said.

We followed the guard back to the van, but I caught a glimpse of someone trying to signal me.

"Eoin, can you distract that guy for a minute?" I whispered.

Nodding, he caught up to the guard and struck up a conversation. I slowed down and knelt as if tying my shoe, and a young woman came closer.

"You're here for Vix?" She barely spoke above a whisper, but it was enough for me to hear the terror in her question.

"I am," I answered. "And anyone else who wants to leave this place."

"I'm Zhora...Vix's friend. I need to get out." She inched closer. "I'll help you if you'll take me with you."

"Of course," I promised. "We'll not leave anyone behind. Pyxis can't claim any of you."

"I wish that were true," she said, her voice so full of pain that I looked up at her as she placed her hands on her stomach. "I'm pregnant with his baby."

FORTY-FIVE
VIX

Today was the twenty-second of September. The Autumn Equinox. The day Pyxis would 'claim me' as his.

Even my usual optimism couldn't find a sliver of hope that things would be okay. There was no escape. I was too well-guarded, and I knew that wouldn't ease up with the ceremony approaching. And even if I could find a way, I wouldn't leave.

Suddenly, the door opened, and I expected the guard. Instead, Zhora stood there.

"I'm here to help you prepare for the ceremony," she said, holding out an ugly red dress.

I felt a stab of betrayal. We used to be like sisters.

As soon as the door shut, her expression changed, and she hurried over to me, her voice barely a whisper.

"I spoke with Carson McCrae."

Warning bells immediately rang. Did Pyxis put her up to this to test me?

But when her hazel eyes met mine, I read the truth there.

"How?"

"He's here. Um, well, was here...this morning." She sat down on the bed next to me. "He and this other guy went to see Pyxis. I had a word with him before he left."

Carson had come for me. Hope flourished. "Did he give you a message?" I almost didn't dare ask.

She smiled. "Oh, there's a lot more than a message."

My heart leaped. "What does that mean?"

"It means we're getting out of here. Your boyfriend has a plan."

I didn't correct her word choice. Carson coming after me was a pretty good sign that our relationship wasn't over.

"What's the plan?"

Zhora glanced at the door again before answering. "He and his brother are here with a group of men to rescue you and Andrea and everyone else who wants to leave."

A lump formed in my throat.

"He said to tell you to be ready at the ceremony. Something will happen then," Zhora said and looked at me. "They're going to rescue us. Aren't they?"

I reached over and took her hand. "I hope so."

She leaned against me, and it felt like we were teenagers again for a moment. "Can I ask you something?"

"Of course," I said.

"What's it like? Outside the commune, I mean." She looked up at me.

I thought for a minute before answering. "It's not that different, honestly. It's not as simple as here. Or at least as simple as it was before Pyxis showed up."

"Would it–" she hesitated, then seemed to gather herself before continuing, "would it be a good place to raise a kid?"

Startled, I looked down at her. "Don't tell me he raped you."

Her lips pressed into a thin line, and she nodded. "At first, it wasn't really like that. I said yes, I wanted to. I'd never been with a man before. Then, after you left, he got...mean. And it just kept getting worse."

I was shocked that Zhora had slept with Pyxis even before I left and never told me.

"I wasn't strong enough to stand up to him like you." She straightened, pulling away from me, her cheeks stained pink.

"Hey, you did nothing wrong." I wrapped my arms around her. "I'm sorry. I could've protected you. Or at least convinced you to come with me."

She hugged me back and then pulled away again, a new squareness to her shoulders. "I *was* scared. *Then*. But now..." she put a hand on her stomach, "I have someone who needs protecting."

"Did Carson say anything else?" I asked.

"Once they interrupt the ceremony, we will have to get out quickly. Use the element of surprise." Then she sighed and stood. "We'll have to talk while we're getting you ready. We can't have anyone getting suspicious."

She was right. I needed to get dressed.

FORTY-SIX
VIX

A SHORT, TIGHT, STRAPLESS DRESS WITH A LOW neckline wasn't anything I expected when Zhora said that she had a dress for me to wear. It looked like something people would wear to a club. It was, well, tacky.

Fortunately, the spiked heels Pyxis wanted me to wear were two sizes too small. Instead, I wore my sandals, which would make it easier for a speedy escape.

"C'mon." The guard didn't hide the impatience in his voice. "Everyone's waiting."

The canopy stood in the commune's center, and I could see everyone gathered underneath it.

My gaze scanned the group for Zhora. In the hour it had taken me to get dressed, Zhora had told a couple of other families who wanted to leave to be ready at any moment. My pulse raced faster when I noticed the armed guards lingering at the edges of the gathering.

Fear was thick in the air, and I felt everyone's eyes

on me as I reached the edge of the canopy. Pyxis, dressed in black slacks and a dark blue shirt, looked like he was going out with friends. All I saw was a monster.

"Wow, baby." His eyes gazed at every inch of my body, not much left to the imagination in the tight dress. "You look smokin'." His voice carried easily since no one, not even the children, made a sound. He held out his hand, his expression daring me to resist. "Come to me."

Every step I took toward Pyxis made my heart pound harder as I refused to doubt Carson. He would be here.

When I reached Pyxis, I took his hand, repressing a shudder. As if he'd sensed it, his grip tightened.

"Before we get started, let's get a few things clear," he said, his voice now so low that only I could hear him. "You're mine. You will serve me in every way I want, whenever I want."

I clenched my teeth hard enough to make my jaw ache. He was provoking me, wanting to see what I'd do. I stayed quiet and simply nodded.

"Good. I was hoping you finally would come around." He yanked on my hand, pulling me closer. "Don't worry. I'll keep my promise that today is just about you and me. I won't claim Andrea…yet." A cruel glint came into his eyes. "But if you so much as look at me cross-eyed, she'll join us in bed that same night."

Fucking bastard.

He continued, "Though I can't say how long I'll be

able to wait. Maybe a year or two. She's growing into quite a sexy little thing, isn't she?"

My control snapped at his disgusting comment, and I pulled my hand from his. Without warning, I balled a fist and drove it into his fucking face.

He staggered backward, shock showing in his eyes before anger. It wouldn't take long for him to retaliate.

Shit.

I took a step back.

"You bitch!" Pyxis shouted, voice blunted and nasal. "I'm going to kill you for that!"

He stepped toward me. I braced myself. He raised his hand, but the sharp crack of a gunshot stopped us all.

FORTY-SEVEN
CARSON

After I spoke with Zhora, I wanted to bust in there as soon as possible, but the plan was to wait until the ceremony to ensure everyone who wanted to leave was present.

When Cain turned a rented van into the commune driveway, I was sweating underneath a bulletproof vest.

"Stop fiddling," Eoin said from the passenger's seat. "You'll be grateful for the vest if one of these assholes gets trigger-happy."

"Head's up," Bruce said from behind us. "It's 'go' time."

In front of me, the two guards came out of the gatehouse, each going to one side of the van like yesterday.

It happened quickly. Cain and Fever hit the men with their doors simultaneously and jumped out. Dez got out of the back with zip ties and made quick work of restraining the guards.

Cain opened the gate, and then our men got back into a second vehicle we'd rented in town a few hours ago.

Cain pulled into the parking lot, and I followed his lead, turning the van around to face the exit, making for a fast escape if we had to. Once parked, we walked around the building, bringing us in sight of the large white canopy right where Zhora said it would be. Even though we couldn't see the details, a few dozen people had gathered under it. Everyone's attention was focused on the far end.

I spotted the white-blonde of Vix's hair next to Pyxis. I had only a moment to register the two of them when Vix hauled off and punched him.

Shit.

"Guys."

I barely had the word out when a gunshot from beside me made me jump. I looked over to find Eoin with one of his handguns pointed over his head. He glanced at me and shrugged.

"Figured that'd get his attention."

He was right. We definitely had *everyone's* attention now.

The guards scrambled to get their guns up, and soon we had a standoff.

"Tell your men to put their guns down, Pyxis," I said, keeping my voice calm and even. "You're outgunned."

"And if I don't?" He stalked toward us, people moving out of the way to let him through. His face was red with anger. "What if I tell them to kill you all?"

"You see that guy?" I gestured toward Fever without looking. "He was a scout sniper in the Army, and his primary focus right now is you. If you don't order your men to stand down, he will put a bullet between your eyes before you can even blink."

"Killing me in cold blood in front of all these witnesses?" Pyxis raised his chin. "I don't think so."

"Try me," I said. "I dare you."

"But my men will die to protect their home and people."

The nervous shuffling of the guards said otherwise. Pyxis may have filled their heads with nonsense about glory and all the sex they could want, but these guys sacrificed nothing for anyone.

"What about your people in the commune?" I asked. "They'd get caught in the crossfire. This is your last chance. Tell your men to stand down, now!"

Fever raised his rifle, and a murmur ran through the crowd, loud enough for us to hear, and Pyxis's arrogant expression faltered.

"Easy now," he said finally. "No need to get all hostile. Put your guns down, men. I'm sure Mr. McCrae and I can come to an agreement that's beneficial to everyone. Perhaps something like we talked about this morning in my office."

I shook my head as the guards moved to obey, and Cain gathered the guns. "That offer no longer stands."

"So you're going to march in here and demand

everyone come with you?" he asked. "Are you going to take them into a corrupt and filthy world where they can be preyed upon by vile politicians and the wealthy who care only for themselves?"

"I'm going to give them a choice," I replied.

"That's the same lie the serpent told the woman," Pyxis said. "He seduced her with temptations of sex and lust and desire, told her that it was her choice to make. That she wouldn't die because of her sins but die, she did–"

"The last time I checked, this was not a religious institution," Vix cut in. She stepped out from behind Pyxis. Wulf, Zhora, and a little girl I assumed was Andrea came with her.

Thankfully, other than the ridiculous dress she wore, she didn't seem any worse for the wear.

"Shut your mouth," Pyxis said, pointing at her. "This man and the outside world have tainted you. We'll not listen to a word you say."

"You don't have to listen," Vix said. "I don't give a damn what you think. All these people need to know is if they disagree with how you're running things, the rules you've made, the things you do, they can come with me and be free of them. Anyone who wants to stay...it's their choice."

"I will not let you do this," Pyxis hissed. He took a step toward Vix, and I reached for my gun.

"Touch me, and you'll have a broken hand to go with that broken nose," she said, narrowing her eyes.

He took a step back, fury written in every line of his face. He turned to the people around him.

"Do you hear how she speaks to me? This *woman*?" He pointed at Vix. "She hit me without provocation. You all saw it. And now she threatened me again."

"This isn't a trial, asshole," Eoin snapped. "Let's get going."

"He's right," Vix said. She looked around at everyone. "We need to leave. Anyone who wants to come with us is welcome, but you have to decide now."

"Follow me," Cain called out before turning and walking back the way we came.

"Go on," Vix said to Wulf and the little girl. "I'll be right behind you."

As Wulf came toward me, his eyes met mine, and he gave me a curt nod. He and I had things we'd talk about later but plenty of time for that. Zhora came right behind the other two, and I noticed the hint of a smile on her face.

It took only a minute before everyone realized we were serious and a handful of girls, none of them looking old enough to vote, came forward. The glances they gave us were wary, and I didn't blame them. They had a significant change ahead of them.

Vix came last, with a man and a woman I guessed from their resemblances to Vix and Wulf to be her parents. She looked at me and smiled, though it didn't quite reach her eyes.

"Is this everyone?" I asked.

She nodded, glancing over her shoulder with a troubled expression. "I'd hoped my sister would come too, but she's staying."

I followed Vix's gaze to a heavyset blonde woman glaring at all of us. "She looks pissed."

"Anise believes nothing bad about Pyxis, no matter what she's heard or seen." Vix sighed. "I can't do anything if she won't listen to reason."

"I'm sorry," I said sincerely.

She shook her head. "I've got everyone who matters. Let's go."

I wanted to say so much more, listen to everything she had to tell me. Just hold her. But this wasn't the time or the place. We still weren't out of danger.

"You heard the lady," Eoin shouted. "Move out."

We backed away, none of us wanting to put our backs to Pyxis or his men. Cain had taken the guards' guns, but no doubt they had more guns stashed away somewhere.

We wouldn't be safe until we were on the road and away from here.

"Do we have enough room?" I asked as soon as I was close enough to the vehicles for Cain to hear me.

"It's going to be tight," he said. "But if we get pulled over, at least we can have an escort to the closest station."

"Where's my brother and niece?" Vix asked.

"In the van," Cain said. "There's space for you there, too."

"Thank you," Vix said. "Seriously. For all of this."

A DRESS FOR CURVES

"We were glad to help," Cain said, before turning to me. "Everyone's in. Let's go."

Vix climbed into the van as Cain got into the SUV. I took the driver's seat, and Vix settled between Eoin and me, the small floor space the only place for her.

"We should've rented another van," Eoin said as he shifted his gun to a better position.

I nodded in agreement but didn't say anything, focused on following Cain out of the parking lot before Vix suddenly made me stop and jumped out.

"Where're you going?" I yelled.

"Sorry, but I'm not losing this again," she said with a big smile as she came out of the guardhouse, her phone in hand. We finally made it out of the gate and down the driveway. My knuckles were white with the force of how hard I grabbed the wheel, and my nerves stretched to snapping. I half-expected to hear gunshots and glass breaking as Pyxis's guards came after us, but they never did.

It wasn't until we were at least a mile away that I let myself breathe easier. As Robert Frost once said, we still had miles to go before we could sleep, but for the moment, we were safe.

FORTY-EIGHT
VIX

"Vix?" A hand on my arm jerked me awake. For a moment, I thought I was back in the commune, then I remembered Carson and his brother rescuing me.

"Hey." I smiled at Carson, hoping to ease the concern on his face. "Sorry. I dozed off for a minute there."

"We're at the police station." His thumb stroked across my skin, sending little tingles of warmth through me.

"I'm ready." Or as much as I could be, anyway.

I opened the door and headed inside to join the others. It surprised me that everybody wanted to press charges against Pyxis and his men. Even my parents, who seemed so reluctant yesterday, sat down with detectives.

"Hey." Eoin spotted us as soon as we stepped

inside and waved us over. "Cain and I figured out a plan from here."

That was good because I had no clue.

"We'll take everybody back to the B&B. Hopefully, they'll have enough rooms. We'll make a couple of trips," he said when a police officer called him for his statement.

For the next several hours, we all gave our statements to the police. I wasn't sure how long I was with Officer Barton, but when I made my way back to the lobby, Carson was already there.

"Everything okay?" he asked as he came toward me.

I nodded. "I gave the apartment landline as my contact number until I get a new phone."

"Dammit." Carson frowned. "I didn't think to ask if we should've grabbed some of your things."

I reached for his hand. "I didn't leave behind anything that couldn't be replaced." I winced at my words as a face flashed into my mind. "None of my things, anyway."

"I'm sorry your sister didn't come." He brushed back a few wisps of hair, his fingertips lingering on my cheek.

"It was her choice," I said. "And that was the whole point, right? To give people choices."

"It doesn't make it any easier to watch when people do the wrong thing," he said.

"I know." I took a deep breath and refocused on the here and now. "Is anyone else done?"

"Most of the men, a few women, and the kids," he said. "Eoin took them over to the B&B a few minutes ago."

"I guess we're waiting for the next group, then." I looked for a chair. "We could be here for a while."

"Actually," Carson looked a little sheepish, "I kinda had Eoin rent a car so you and I could have a little more freedom to move around, just the two of us...if that's what you want, of course."

"I'd love to," I said. "I think we should talk, too. In fact, can you take me home?"

"Home?" Carson asked, confused.

"Take me to your apartment."

Carson's eyes widened. "Absolutely."

After informing my family I was leaving with Carson, he held out his hand, and I didn't hesitate. The strength of his fingers as they closed over mine, the heat of his skin, all of it felt right. Like I clicked into a place I'd been jostled out of.

I was on my way home.

FORTY-NINE
CARSON

I WAS RELIEVED WHEN VIX HAD AGREED TO COME with me. Vix had fallen asleep during the four-hour drive, but we were almost home. Everything was falling into place, finally.

But, as I entered the garage, I got nervous all over again. The conversation I wanted to have was only minutes away, and I had no idea how to express the crazy rush of emotions I felt.

Her fingers laced with mine as we walked to the elevator gave me hope. Maybe I hadn't lost her.

"It feels good to be back in the city," she said, looking out the windows as we entered the apartment.

"I'm sorry I behaved like an ass before you left," I blurted out. "I should've done things differently. Listened to you. Talked things through logically rather than letting my emotions get the better of me."

"Don't be. It's me who should say sorry," she said.

That surprised me. I squeezed her hand.

"You did nothing wrong. I pushed you away on purpose, Carson. But I had to. It was the only way I could make myself go. I should have talked to you instead of letting my fear become helplessness, thinking I had no other choice but to go along with what Pyxis wanted."

"Helpless isn't a word I would use to describe you," I said with a small smile. "But next time you're planning something dangerous, please let me help you."

"I like the sound of that." She smiled softly.

My heart was pounding. "I love you, Vix," I said. "And I don't say those words lightly."

"I love you, too." She put her hands on my chest. Our gazes held in silence for seconds before we moved, mouths colliding with bruising force. Her hands on my neck, nails scratching at the base of my skull. I buried my fingers in her hair, the pale strands like silk. A growl escaped me as she pressed her body against mine, all of her soft places fitting perfectly against my harder ones.

We were both wearing too many clothes.

I took a step back, letting my gaze slide down her body...and couldn't stop myself from laughing. Not a lot, but it was clearly a laugh.

"Please tell me that isn't your dress."

Vix's puzzlement turned to amusement. "Hell, no. This thing is a sorry excuse for a dress."

"Well, then..." I ran a finger along the low neckline, the tip whisking her bare skin. She shivered, lips parting in the most tempting manner.

"It's not very well made," I said, studying the dress carefully. "The slightest bit of pressure in the right place and...." I let my voice trail off as I raised my eyes to meet Vix's.

Her pupils dilated, and her voice came out breathless as she asked, "And what?"

"I could literally tear your clothes off."

She inhaled a sharp breath, and with a jerk of my hand, I tore it straight down the middle. Falling to the ground, it revealed gorgeous, full breasts and a tiny pair of red panties.

Damn.

I cupped her breasts and enjoyed the weight of them, the heat of her skin. I blew on her, and her pale nipples tightened. I flicked the tip with my tongue, and she made a slight sound that went straight to my cock.

"You have the most amazing tits," I muttered.

She laughed, the sound turning into a moan as I took a nipple into my mouth. The taste of her skin was familiar and addictive. I sucked on it slowly, and deep pulls had her crying out. When I turned to the other one, I slid a hand around to her fine ass. I teased her nipple with my teeth while I squeezed the firm flesh.

There were so many things I wanted to do to that ass.

She tugged on my hair until I raised my head. "Bed?"

I caught her mouth in a kiss before answering, "Get comfortable. I'm going to take your panties off with my teeth."

"I hope you have additional plans for your mouth after that," she teased as she kicked the dress away.

I watched her step out of her sandals and walk to the bed, hips swaying with every step.

Damn.

My pants were now uncomfortably tight. Then Vix sat on the edge and spread her legs, showing how very little that red fabric covered.

"You know, before you come over here, I think it's only fair I get a show like you did."

"You want to tear my clothes off?" I raised an eyebrow. "I'm game for it, but the jeans might be difficult."

She shook her head, her fingers slowly trailing down between her breasts, over her stomach, and then to the waistband of her panties. "I'd prefer to watch you undress…slowly."

"And while I do that?" I asked, eyeing her hand.

"I'm going to enjoy it." Her fingers slipped just under the edge of her underwear and then stopped, waiting.

"I almost wish I was wearing more layers," I said as I grabbed the bottom of my shirt and drew it up my torso. I pulled it over my head and tossed it onto the nearby chair.

"Mm. I like that idea." She wet her bottom lip. "I can think of a few fantasies that we could act out. A fireman has many layers."

I suppressed a groan as I watched her hand moving, imagined the slick, wet heat of her against my fingers, the tight grip of her pussy when I slid my digits inside, the silk of the even more sensitive skin of her clit.

"Hey, don't get distracted. You're supposed to be giving me a show, remember?"

"All right." I gave her my most wicked smile and unsnapped my jeans. The bulge from my erection strained against my boxer briefs to get free, but I deliberately took my time to test her patience.

"Carson..." The warning in her tone made me grin.

"I'm just doing what you asked. Taking my clothes off slowly."

She glared at me, but the moment my hands went to my waist, her gaze dropped, her breathing coming faster as she waited for me to continue.

I lowered my jeans over my hips and thighs, feeling the heat of Vix's eyes follow me the entire way. Tossing my jeans toward my shirt, I straightened.

"Turn around." The order was breathless enough to tell me she was close to orgasm.

"Touch yourself," she said. "I wanna come while I watch."

I faced her again, my cock rock hard. I shoved my hand into my underwear, gripping the shaft tight. The air hissed out from between my teeth, and I clenched every muscle to stop myself from coming right then.

Her free hand trailed up her stomach, and my eyes followed. She cupped her breast, teasing her nipple with her fingers. She moaned as she tugged on the sensitive flesh. "Take out your cock, please."

"Since you asked so nicely." My voice was rough as I freed my throbbing cock.

She let out a curse, her hand shifting in such a way that I knew she'd plunged at least one finger, if not two, inside her. My dick ached to be inside her, to feel her gripping me, milking every drop of pleasure from me.

"Fuck," I growled the word. "Do you have any idea how hot you are?"

Her breasts heaved as her breathing quickened, and her hand moved faster.

"After you come, I'll lick you into another orgasm," I promised. "And then I'm going to fuck you until you come again. You look so sweet when you come."

As she writhed on the bed, her fingers working between her legs, I had to squeeze the base of my cock to keep from losing it.

"How will you take me?" she asked.

"How do you want it?" I took a step toward the bed. "Missionary? From behind? On top? It's the lady's choice."

Her eyes met mine. "I want to ride you."

I groaned. "Fuck, Vix. You're going to make me come before I even get to the bed."

"How much do you want me?" she asked. "Tell me how much."

"More than anything," I said. "I think about you all the time. I can't stop. And I want you all the time. I think about how I want to make love to you. Spend hours worshiping your body. Fucking you hard and fast against a wall. Just the sight of you makes me hard." I took another step toward her. "I've wanted you from the moment you walked into my studio, and I haven't stopped."

She came with a small cry, her body tightening, eyes squeezing shut. By the time she opened them, I'd rid myself of my underwear and was on my knees between her legs. Running my fingers up her body, I hooked my fingers into the waistband and tugged off her panties.

I nipped at the inside of her thigh to be sure I had her attention and then pressed my mouth against her soft, sensitive skin. My tongue parted her lips, swiping from core to clit and reveling in the taste of her. When my tongue reached that bundle of nerves, her hips jerked. I grabbed onto them, holding her in place as I repeated the motion twice more. As tempting as it was to take my time and savor her, my need for her had stretched my self-control to its limit.

I brought her quickly with my mouth, using everything I learned she liked. A hint of teeth. My tongue on her clit, then my fingers curled inside to rub against her g-spot. The combination of the two motions...and she came with a scream.

As she fell back onto the bed, body limp, I got to my feet. While she recovered, I retrieved a condom from my bag. After rolling it on, I joined Vix on the bed, stretching out next to her.

"Wow," she said finally. She rolled onto her side to face me. "That was...wow."

"Thanks." I chuckled. Reaching over, I twisted a lock of hair around my finger. "It was my pleasure."

She shook her head and pushed herself up on her knees. "I think that was more *my pleasure*. Your turn."

Giving me a slight push, she moved me onto my back and swung her leg over my waist. Taking me in hand, she held my cock still as she slowly lowered herself.

I cursed as I slid inside her, the tight heat almost too much. Fisting the blanket, I let out a groan. My eyes wanted to close, but I forced them to stay open, wanting to watch her. As she began to move, sensations rocked me to the core. Every nerve was on fire as I fought back my release.

Vix moaned, playing with her nipples as she rode me. I could feel her thighs quivering against my hips, signaling that she was close to climax again. I grasped her hips and pushed up into her, taking her deeper, harder. She let out a cry, her hands dropping to my stomach. Her nails dug into my skin, the bite of pain drawing a curse out of me. I wouldn't last much longer. Dropping my hand to where our bodies were joined, I found her clit. A little pressure on that swollen bundle and she went stiff, her back arching, mouth opening wide in a soundless keen. When she tightened around me, sending me over the edge, only one thought was on my mind.

No matter where I was, as long as I was with her, I was home.

FIFTY

VIX

The sun was blinding me when I opened my eyes. Not only that, the surroundings were unfamiliar. Then it all came back to me. I was in Carson's apartment.

I rolled to my side and squinted at the clock sitting on the bedside table.

Geez, I slept until ten.

I looked to the other side of the bed, but it was empty except for a note on the pillow.

I raised up on an elbow to reach it, smiled, and pulled the covers under my chin, feeling safe. How sweet. He left me a note. It said he had an early business meeting with his assistant, Louis, and a client, but he promised to be back before noon. And he signed it, "Miss you, already."

My first love note. We didn't have those in the commune, but I liked it this way. Traditional relationships were becoming more appealing to me.

I sat up and swung my legs off the bed, pausing for a moment. I'd left the commune with nothing but my phone.

I sighed and laid the note on the bedside table. As I headed for the shower, I glanced at the hideous red dress I'd been forced to wear at the ceremony. Having to wear it again almost made me throw up. But I didn't have my clothes.

That's when my eye caught something sitting on the top of the dresser. I walked over to find underwear, jeans, a top, shoes, and socks, all in my size.

There was even a small purse.

Oh, the perks of having a fashion designer for a boyfriend. What else could I possibly ask for?

I was practically singing as I stepped into the shower.

My life was back on track. Almost. I had a few things to clear up today. I needed to call Susanna and let her know I was okay. Then find out about my job. Maybe if I begged Dasia and Yasmin for my old job back, they would consider it.

I wouldn't blame them if they told me to forget it. In the end, I left without telling them anything.

After my shower, I dressed, hoping no one would notice I was wearing men's deodorant and tucked my love note into my new purse. I grabbed my phone from the nightstand, then headed to the kitchen.

I rummaged through the refrigerator and decided on a bottle of water before calling Susanna. I took a long drink as I moved to the living room, dropped onto the couch, and pulled Susanna's number.

"Vix!" Susanna practically shouted. "Where are you? What happened? Are you okay? I've been worried to death! Tell me you're okay...are you hurt? You didn't answer my calls."

"Slow down, Susanna. Yes, yes, I'm okay. Take a breath." I chuckled.

"Are you in the hospital? I've been calling. You didn't answer, and I thought you were dead or something...."

"Susanna! Stop with the rapid-fire questions already. I'm okay. I'm not hurt. I'm not in the hospital. I'm safe at Carson's apartment."

"Oh, thank God. So Carson found you...."

"Yes, thanks to you."

"Me?"

"The information you gave Carson was part of the clues he needed to find the commune." I paused. "I realize now I should've talked more about my previous life. But it was easier to forget my childhood home than feel the pain of missing it."

"Aw, Vix, I wish you'd have told me more. So what happened? Why did you go back to the commune?"

"Well, it's a long story that needs to be told over a girl's night out like we used to do. But, Susanna, I can't thank you enough. If you hadn't told Carson what you knew. I..." My voice got thick, and I had to swallow.

"Don't worry about it. I'm here for you, Vix. Always. And if you ever want to come back as my roommate, I've got you covered. Karen Devereaux can go fuck herself." She laughed.

Just then, I heard the front door of the apartment open.

"Hey, Susanna, Carson just came home. I gotta go. But let's set a date for a get-together, and I'll fill you in on everything."

"No worries. You two have fun. I'm sure you want to spend time with him. I'll call you in a couple of days to set something up."

I ended the call and left my phone on the couch.

"Let me help you with that." I jumped up to meet Carson as he came through the door, balancing several takeout boxes and a bag.

"Thanks. I got waffles!" He grinned. "I think you said they're your favorite."

I grabbed a box, and we brought the food to the kitchen table.

"I'm starving. Oh, my god. How much food did you get? It looks like you went a little overboard."

He laughed as he opened the boxes. There were waffles with strawberries and cream, chocolate croissants, scrambled eggs, bacon, *and* sausage.

We slid into the chairs and started eating.

"Oh, wow. You're right. This waffle is to die for," I said after my first bite.

Carson grinned. "This place has the best breakfasts."

There was another bag sitting on the countertop, and I pointed at it with my fork. "What's in that?"

"Bagels and cream cheese. I wasn't sure if you wanted croissants or bagels, so what the hell. I got both...." He speared a bite of waffle and stuffed it in his mouth, still grinning. He hadn't stopped smiling since he came in. I guess he was feeling as happy as I was.

"So, what are your plans for today besides just being your beautiful self?"

I furrowed my brow. "Well..." I set my fork on the edge of my plate. "I need to go to the boutique and see if Yasmin and Dasia would consider rehiring me. I'm not very hopeful, considering I left them in the lurch."

"I think you'll be fine. They really like you."

We finished our breakfast, and Carson kissed me goodbye as he left for his studio.

I took one last look around the kitchen before leaving and noticed the apartment keys I'd left behind sitting on the counter in a corner. I snagged them for later and headed out to catch a cab.

MY NERVES WERE CHATTERING as I approached the boutique. I paused outside the door and smoothed down my shirt. I had no idea what would greet me when I saw Yasmin and Dasia, but I had nothing to lose and everything to win.

The second I stepped inside the boutique, I noticed how busy it was. Yasmin caught my eye, and a broad smile broke out on her face. "Vix!" She came forward to give me a big hug. "I'm so glad to see you!"

She turned and called out to the back room. "Dasia, Dasia, come. Vix is here!"

Dasia poked her head out, offered another big smile, and embraced me. "We were worried about you. Carson told us you had to leave. Something about your niece."

I was glad to hear Carson had filled them in a little. "Everything turned out well, thank god. Carson was a lifesaver. I wouldn't be here if it hadn't been for him. But enough about me. I see you are busy." I waved a hand.

"Ever since Carson's show, it's been insane," Dasia said. "We're the only boutique that carries his complete line."

Just then, a woman interrupted and asked if she could try on a dress.

Dasia replied to her. "Yes, of course." She turned to us and said, "I'll go help her."

"I'm sorry to barge in unannounced, but I was afraid I might lose my nerve if I didn't just come in," I said to Yasmin

She looked puzzled. "For what?"

"I was hoping you might rehire me. I know it's asking a lot since I left without notice but...."

Yasmin cut me off. "Are you kiddin'? Girl, you'll always have a job here for as long as you want."

Another customer interrupted, holding a blue dress on a hanger, and asked for a size fourteen.

I looked at Yasmin, who nodded, then I took the dress from the customer as I smiled and said, "Yes, it comes in size fourteen. Let me show you." I took her to the rack of dresses, pointing out the fine quality of the dress she had chosen as we walked.

And just like that, I was working again.

After the rush of customers died down, I sat down on the high stool behind the front counter. "Whew. Was that the after-lunch rush? You were right when you said business has picked up, " I said to Dasia.

"I'm not complaining." She smiled.

I heard a ping from my phone. I'd tucked it in my new purse under the counter for safekeeping.

I smiled as I saw the notification. It was a text from Carson.

Don't make plans for tonight. We're going out.

My heart was warm as I replied: *I'm all yours.*

I was with the man I loved and had the job I loved again. What more could possibly happen?

I jumped off the stool and joined Yasmin and Dasia.

"Is it okay if I take off now? With all the craziness going on since yesterday, I haven't even been back to my apartment yet."

"Of course," Dasia said. "We'll work up a schedule for you. You were a big help today."

I collected my purse and slung the strap across my body before heading out the door to go home and get ready for tonight. Luckily, I'd left the clothes Carson gave me in the closet so I'd have something nice to wear.

Outside, I was about to hail a cab when I saw the

sign for the subway. I froze, then blew out a breath. Maybe it was time. Like they say, if you fall off a horse…

If I could stand up to Pyxis, facing the subway would be a piece of cake. I headed for the entrance and walked down the stairs.

FIFTY-ONE
CARSON

We were at a local Italian restaurant, one of my favorites, where the service is top-notch, and everybody knows me by name. The lights were dim, and soft music filled the room, giving the place a cozy, romantic ambiance. A candle and a single rose decorated the linen-covered table.

"You're spoiling me. This tastes like heaven, and it's so tender," Vix said as she took another bite of her food. "What is it again?"

"It's Osso Buco," I said with a smile. Looking at Vix across the table was a dream come true. I was the luckiest man in the world to have found her and to think I'd almost lost her.

"It's oh-so good," she said with a laugh. "We didn't have food like this in the commune."

I smiled and said, "I love your innocence, and I can't wait to introduce you to so much amazing food. But, before I forget, I have another show coming up next month, and I think we should try something new for your next dress to model."

Vix slumped in her chair as she dropped her fork, and sighed. "I'm not sure I have what it takes to be a model, honestly. Why would anyone want to look at me? I know you really like me, but I'm not a professional model." She shrugged.

"You must be joking," I said and pulled out my phone. "Have you not seen this?" I passed my phone to Vix. "It's an article about my show from Fashion Insider magazine. Scroll to the picture and read the caption."

Vix read it out loud. "New era of fashion models. Vixen Teal steals the show." She looked up from the phone, her eyes wide. "What?"

"You're a hit. Louis has been getting calls from modeling agencies asking who is representing you."

"Really? They're asking about me? I can't believe it."

"Louis wants to be your manager and help you find the right agency."

"I don't know what to say other than…wow!" She laughed.

When the waiter brought a giant piece of Chocolate Volcano cake with ice cream, whipped cream, and fudge sauce, Vix's eyes went wide. "Just when I thought things couldn't get better," she laughed again. A sound I would never tire of.

Vix picked up her spoon. "This is over the top decadent. Good thing we are sharing a piece."

"Only the best for you." I took her hand and kissed the back of it before we dug in.

After a few bites, I placed my spoon on the table and said, "I have one slight problem. I need the apartment you're using back for a month. A model from England is coming to town, and I'd promised her months ago she could stay there."

"Oh, that's no problem. I can probably stay with Susanna."

I grabbed something from my pocket. "I have a better idea." She looked straight at me. "Come stay with me. We can do a trial for a month. If living together doesn't work out, you can have the apartment back when Samantha leaves." I opened my hand. "I already had a key made for you, hoping you would say yes."

I placed it in front of her on the fine linen tablecloth as I held my breath.

She picked it up. "It's a little soon, but...what the heck. Under one condition...that we can have breakfast delivered from the waffle deli every morning." She gave me a big smile.

"Baby, I can promise a lot more than waffles every morning."

EPILOGUE

Vix

"Seriously, Vix, don't you have a date?" Yasmin asked. "It's your birthday. You can't let your man wait. He's about to spoil you rotten."

"Oh, he spoils me every day." I gave her a wicked smile and handed her the felt-tip marker. "Let me just say hi to Susanna."

"Sure, hun. Susanna's in the back," she said and left me to greet a new customer.

I glanced at the poster Yasmin had insisted I autographed the moment I'd set foot in the door.

It was ironic.

Despite no longer working here, I would still be here every day, in the shape of a five-foot poster hanging behind the desk. It featured me in the latest Carson McCrae dress, made with Chinese silk in a beautiful turquoise color.

It was the perfect dress for spring weather.

I pushed the thoughts aside and opened the door to the backroom.

"There's my celebrity birthday girl. Happy Birthday, Vix." Susanna was ecstatic as she gave me a big hug.

When Louis negotiated a contract with Manhattan Models for me, I realized I had to give up my job at the boutique. But I'd left my job in the best hands. It had taken Susanna less than half a second to depart the Devereauxes and accept the job as my replacement. Not only that, Stellan was now helping her gain refugee status and apply for citizenship. It was a fresh start with a real future, and I couldn't be more excited for her.

We chatted for a few minutes before I had to get going.

Already late, I took a cab home, and as the driver navigated the slow-moving traffic of a Manhattan afternoon, I recalled the events since the day Carson saved me.

The police arrested Pyxis two days after all the reports were filed on charges of kidnapping, false imprisonment, assault, and rape. Numerous counts of each. And other charges were pending as the authorities looked into his buddies and their many weapons. The judge set an astronomical bail, and no one paid it, so he and his friends were still in prison.

Zhora had found a boyfriend, a nice guy. And she wasn't the only one from the commune doing well, either. Carson helped find Wulf and Andrea an apartment close to us, making it easy to help get them acclimated to living in the city. My parents and I were still mending our relationship. It took me a while to admit how much their refusal to stand up to Pyxis had hurt me.

None of the people who stayed at the commune, even Anise, would talk to us.

I hoped, eventually, she would come to her senses. Phina missed her, but I had little hope of finding a relationship with my sister.

Soon after we came back from the commune, Detective Kozuch called Carson about the muggers from the subway. The police believed they had found the two with the help of the surveillance footage, but I needed to pick them out in a lineup. I wasn't sure I would recognize them since the assault had happened so fast, but the minute I saw the people in the line, I could identify both without a doubt. I never got my purse or wallet back, but at least the robbers were no longer on the street.

Finally, I got home and hurried to get dressed.

"God, you're beautiful," Carson said as I stood in just a bra and panties. He was looking insanely hot in his suit and tie, the latter of which was the same shade of baby blue as his eyes. "I'm tempted to say to hell with dinner and stay here." He crossed the room and took my hand, brushing his lips across my knuckles.

"We could just be late," I suggested, warmth coiling in my belly.

"I'm afraid Scaline Fabiani will give away our reservation if we're not there on time." He squeezed my hand. "How about we look at dinner as necessary fuel for a long night of making love and multiple orgasms?"

I chuckled, gave him a light kiss, and headed for the bathroom. "I like the sound of that."

Ten minutes later, I took a last look in the mirror and admired my favorite Carson McCrae design. The dress that Brietta Devereaux almost ruined with a glass of wine. Thanks to Derry's quick thinking, it looked as good as new.

"The car's waiting," he said as he popped in the doorway with his charming smile. I still wanted to rip off his clothes right there, but we made it out of the apartment and down to the street, fully clothed.

"You're not driving tonight?"

He shook his head. "I enjoy riding in the back with you, whispering everything I want to do to you, knowing you're getting wet."

I swallowed hard. It still surprised me the things Carson said. No one really got to know the man whose way with words could turn me on in seconds.

Damn, I loved this man.

"You're going to get me all hot and bothered before dinner?" I shook my head. "Such a wicked man."

He laughed, and the sound made me shiver. "I promise to behave on my way there. I can't speak to what happens *after* that."

True to his word, Carson behaved himself from the

moment we got into the car's back seat until our waiter came to ask for our dessert orders.

While indulging in a delicious chocolate supreme brownie with a scoop of ice cream, we talked about work and our families, and plans for the upcoming week. Then he surprised me by asking what I thought about visiting Scotland. I knew he had some extended family there, but he never talked about it much.

"That would be wonderful," I said. "Do you have any specific date in mind?"

"I was thinking we could decide together." He took a deep breath, reached into his pocket, and pulled out a small square box. "Since it would be for our honeymoon."

My breath caught as I stared at the box. Was he really doing this? Here? Now?

He opened it to reveal the most beautiful ring I'd ever seen. On a gold band, tiny amethysts made flower petals, and at the center was a diamond. He rose from the chair, got down on one knee, and asked the question.

"Vixen Teal, will you marry me?"

"Yes!" The word burst out of me, louder than intended. The surrounding people broke into applause as Carson slid the ring onto my finger. He came around the table and bent down to kiss me. I reached up, running my fingers through those soft curls.

"I want you naked," he whispered against my lips. "Wearing nothing but that ring as I make you come hard enough to see stars."

I nodded. "And I want my hand on your cock so you can feel the metal against your skin as I stroke you right up to the edge."

His eyes widened, and he straightened. "Check, please."

THE END

THE SCOTTISH BILLIONAIRES READING ORDER

SEASON 1:

Alec & Lumen:
Prequel
1. Off Limits
2. Breaking Rules
3. Mending Fate

Eoin & Aline:
1. Strangers in Love
2. Dangers of Love

Brody & Freedom:
1. Single Malt
2. Perfect Blend

SEASON 2:

THE SCOTTISH BILLIONAIRES READING ORDER

Baylen & Harlee:
Business or Pleasure

Drake & Maggie:
At First Sight

Carson & Vix:
A Dress for Curves

Cireon & Christina:
Bad Press

Printed in Great Britain
by Amazon